The
TRAGEDY
of
MACBETH

—

PART II

The Seed of Banquo

The
TRAGEDY
of
MACBETH

PART II
The Seed of Banquo

❧ ❧

NOAH
LUKEMAN

PEGASUS BOOKS
NEW YORK

THE TRAGEDY OF MACBETH, PART II
THE SEED OF BANQUO

Pegasus Books LLC
80 Broad Street, 5th Floor
New York, NY 10004

First Pegasus Books cloth edition 2008
First Pegasus Books trade paperback edition 2010

Interior design by Simon Sullivan

Library of Congress Cataloging-in-Publication Data is available.

ISBN: 978-1-60598-079-9

10 9 8 7 8 6 5 4 3 2 1

Printed in the United States of America
Distributed by W. W. Norton & Company, Inc.
www.pegasusbooks.us

INTRODUCTION

Some time ago, I set out to adapt *Macbeth* for the screen and spent months dissecting the text, grappling with every line and word. While contemplating both the opening (the witches' prophecy) and the conclusion (Malcolm's ascent as king), I was struck by a realization: *Macbeth* is unfinished. The prophecy which initiates the play's action proclaims first that Macbeth will be king and then that Banquo's children will be kings. Macbeth indeed becomes Scotland's king—and yet Banquo's prophecy remains unfulfilled. The play ends, oddly, with Banquo's seed nowhere in sight and with a third party, Malcolm, ascending to the throne.

One might argue that not all of the witches' prophecies were meant to come to pass. Yet throughout *Macbeth* the witches' other prophecies, no matter how twisted, are all fulfilled on stage (even Birnam Wood manages to "move" as they predict). One might argue that Banquo's prophecy is insignificant, a mere historical footnote in the play. Yet if this were the case, why would Shakespeare go to such lengths to dramatize a scene in which Banquo is murdered and his child, Fleance, escapes (thus leaving the door open for his future ascent)? The prophecy regarding Banquo's child is, in fact, ubiquitous in the play, as Macbeth dwells obsessively on the ascent of "the seed of Banquo." Indeed, the very reason Macbeth cannot find peace as king is because his mind is fixated on the moment when

Banquo's prophecy will come to pass, when Banquo's seed will take his throne.

One might, then, try to dismiss all of this as merely an oversight by Shakespeare, argue that he simply forgot to resolve this particular plot line in the play. But would the greatest of English dramatists, who was careful with every syllable, actually neglect to resolve an entire subplot, indeed, the very driving action of his play? If not, then did he have something else in mind? Could he have been preparing for a *Macbeth, Part II*?

Struck by this possibility, I went back and reanalyzed the text of *Macbeth*, looking for any other clues that might point to Shakespeare's preparing a sequel. I was shocked to discover two more compelling pieces of evidence. The first appears in Lady Macbeth's famous monologue: "I have given suck and know/How tender 'tis to love the babe that milks me." In this line, she tells us that she has a child. But then where is the child Macbeth? Why is he/she omitted from the play? Is the only child of a king and queen, the sole heir to the throne, so insignificant as to not merit any other mention?

The other hint came in the character of Prince Donalbain (Malcolm's brother). After their father, Duncan, is murdered by Macbeth, the two princes, both legitimately in line for the throne, agree to flee for safety's sake in two directions: Malcolm, to England; Donalbain, to Ireland. Yet when Malcolm returns to oust Macbeth, Donalbain, oddly, does not join him. And when Malcolm ascends to the throne at the play's end, his prince brother is nowhere in sight. Why would Shakespeare keep Donalbain in Ireland? And why end *Macbeth* on this note?

Was Shakespeare thrice careless? Or could the playwright known for multipart plays (*Henry IV, Part I* and *II*, *Henry VI, Part I, II* and *III*), have also had in mind a *Macbeth, Part II*?

The concept haunted me. The more I thought about it, the

more I felt that these plot elements were substantial enough to justify a play in their own right: an unfulfilled prophecy; a child Macbeth; a boy destined to be king; the princely Donalbain suspiciously in Ireland while his brother sits on the Scottish throne; the newly crowned Malcolm, the bereft Macduff, the devious Seyton. And, of course, the three witches. They are, in fact, among a very rare group of villains whom Shakespeare leaves to live another day.

I pondered what medium could best suit such a sequel. I could not envision a sequel to *Macbeth* written in contemporary English or in the form of a novel. Too much would be lost in the conversion process; it would become something else. Any attempt at a sequel, I felt, should be as true to its Shakespearean model as possible. I concluded that it should appear in the same form as *Macbeth*: as a play, in the traditional Shakespearean five-act structure, in Elizabethan English, and in blank verse.

It obviously took much more deliberation before I could summon the resolve to go forth. Despite my enthusiasm for the concept, I had an enormously hard time with the idea of approaching Shakespeare's work. It felt like sacrilege. Then I thought long and hard of Shakespeare's life, and realized that when he himself—a slightly-educated, minor actor—attempted to write a play, he was excoriated, brandished an "upstart crow," criticized for even daring to attempt to write in blank verse (supposedly to be reserved only for those with a university education). As Ben Johnson said, he "had small Latin, and less Greek."

But this was precisely his virtue. Shakespeare was not a scholar, and he did not write for the academic elite. He was of the people. Undeterred by the rigid societal pressure of "what should be" and "what shouldn't be," he followed what was, for him, a more important route: pursuing his artistic vision with fervor, whatever the consequence. Qualified or not, he jumped in and attempted something brash. I think that Shakespeare (as both actor and writer) would, with a wink, be the first to encourage someone to attempt a *Macbeth, Part II*.

The Tragedy of Macbeth, Part II is not a scholarly endeavor; it is an artistic one, meant both to pick up where *Macbeth* left off and to stand as a complete play in its own right. It is my hope that it will be enjoyed by actors, directors, and theater companies eager to grapple with a new text, to play new roles, and by theatergoers eager to watch them. So many people around the world love the cadences of blank verse. Yet there has been scarce new material for 400 years.

I think it's time we gave them something.

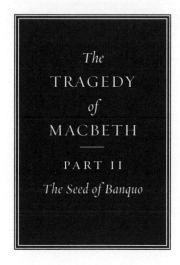

The
TRAGEDY
of
MACBETH
———
PART II
The Seed of Banquo

For Banquo's issue have I filed my mind;
For *them* the gracious Duncan have I murder'd . . .
Only for them . . .
To make *them* kings, the seed of Banquo kings!

—Macbeth

Year

1060

Dramatis Personae

MALCOLM

MACDUFF

SEYTON

SIWARD

LENNOX

ANGUS

ROSS

DONALBAIN

FLEANCE

CAWDOR

LADY MALCOLM

NURSE

FIONA

SYNA

DOCTOR

PORTER

THREE WITCHES

(cont'd)

THREE MURDERERS

TWO PETITIONERS

SUITOR

SUITOR'S FATHER

TWO GUARDS

SIX CROWD MEMBERS

ATTENDANTS

MESSENGERS

GHOST OF MACBETH

GHOST OF BANQUO

ACT · I

SCENE I

Heath at sunset.

Enter Three Witches.

FIRST WITCH Now that we three meet again,
  No thunder, lightning, absent rain.

SECOND WITCH No wars that rage, no plague that spreads,
  no envied crown, no sleepless beds.

THIRD WITCH The hurly-burly now is done,
  the battle has been lost and won.

ALL Sink down, now, the setting sun.

FIRST WITCH Invite a fog, let it rise,
  bring for Malcolm slow demise.

SECOND WITCH A lizard's eye, a drop of sage,
  lend this Malcolm baseless rage.

THIRD WITCH A tiger's claw, berries tart,
  seal this king a blackened heart.

FIRST WITCH An eagle's spine, a cup of sand,
  spark new wars throughout the land.

ALL Fair is foul, and foul is fair,
  Hover in fog and filthy air.   *Exeunt.*

SCENE II

Dunsinane.
Malcolm, seated, with Attendants.

Enter Macduff, Seyton, Siward, Lennox, Angus and Attendants.

ALL God save the King!

MALCOLM Welcome, dear counsel. But why such haste?

LENNOX   My liege,
    a band of men has formed about Fleance.

ANGUS They head for the sea.

SEYTON   'Tis a dangerous mob,
    and it will swell before it touches the shore.

MALCOLM Fleance then rebuffed our invitation?

LENNOX He said he would ne'er again grace the walls
    of Dunsinane.

SEYTON   'Tis a sharp rebuke,
    the prologue to some greater action. We must
    strike now, before this worm becomes a snake.

MALCOLM Macduff, you are silent.

MACDUFF   Forgive, my lord. It is
    my language since the murder of the ones
    I loved.

MALCOLM Shall we strike Fleance?

MACDUFF   No, my lord.

SEYTON   Traitor!
                                                Macduff draws.

MACDUFF This sword will take your head as swift as took
   it Macbeth's.

MALCOLM   Stay, Macduff. Seyton, allow his speech.

MACDUFF Fleance's gathering is but a few dozen souls.
   They pose no threat to your great throne. They head
   away from Dunsinane, not towards.

SEYTON   In order to regroup
   on some other shore.

MACDUFF   You are a mighty
   king, my liege. You have no reason to fear
   an absconding boy.

SEYTON   This boy is now a man,
   and thinks manly thoughts.

MACDUFF   Shall Scotland see
   a king grown so uncertain of his throne
   that he'd unleash an army 'gainst a pack
   of men?

SEYTON   Shall Scotland watch a king afraid
   to stop rebellion in his midst?   *A cheer.*

MALCOLM What noise is that outside my window?

ANGUS   A throng
   has camped to celebrate your reign. 'Tis ten
   years today since your ascent.

MALCOLM Is it today? Then this day also marks
the anniversary of Macbeth's fall.
O, two-headed day! God has graced
us with ten quiet years. Scotland thrives;
Norway dares not attack; and the reign
of the Macbeths doth fade from memory.
The land now lies content, except in its need
of an heir, which I will soon provide. Stalk
Fleance; but do not attack. He has
commited no crime. Graver the danger that I
become the likeness of Macbeth than that
a boy-man dream of breaching Dunsinane.

SEYTON   My lord,
the danger lies not in Fleance's present strength;
it lies in the prophecy that he, not you,
shall inherit Scotland's throne.

MALCOLM Let us declare our days of prophecy
concluded. Scotland has prospered without such dark
omens, and the witches' words have proved false.

SEYTON But, my liege—

MALCOLM   I have spoken.

Enter Ross.

ROSS God save the King.

MALCOLM What news from Ireland?
How fares my dear brother?

ROSS   News which shames
me to report, my lord. A massive army
forms 'round Donalbain.

MALCOLM   For what purpose?

ROSS I know not, and thus urge temperance.
　Yet a host of ships rests on their shore,
　and they all point towards Scotland.

SIWARD   What!

SEYTON Traitor!

LENNOX   Villain!

MALCOLM   Even so?

ROSS   We do not know
　their purpose, my lord.

MACDUFF   Ships set on a shore
　do not in themselves prove ill intent.

SIWARD What other intent could there be?

LENNOX   If peaceful,
　he would have forewarned.

MACDUFF   Perhaps it was gathered in haste.

SEYTON In haste to conquer Dunsinane.
　You would have Donalbain's army pounding
　on our gates and wonder at his intent.

MALCOLM Enough! Are not my brother and I two halves
　of one same Duncan? I cannot imagine
　he aims for my throne.

MACDUFF   He is a noble soul,
　kind, valiant, honest.

MALCOLM   Yet 'tis strange
  he never returned to Scotland.

SEYTON But 'tis not,
  my lord: for if your brother was devoid
  of princely ambition, surely he would have returned,
  as one brother to another, to the land
  of his birth. If he lacked the lust
  for power, he would have warned of his intent—
  indeed, would not have massed such arms. The truest
  villain does not reveal himself until
  the moment meet for his desire—
  and for this the truest will wait a lifetime.

MALCOLM Proceed to Ireland, noble Ross. Tell
  my brother to return to Scotland at once, alone,
  so that I may interrogate his intent.   *Exit Ross.*

SEYTON It is a fool's errand, my lord. He will
  return, but with men in tow. We must prepare
  a defense, not grant him time to launch.

MALCOLM I have spoken. Go to.   *Exeunt.*

MALCOLM   Macduff?   *Macduff remains.*

MALCOLM You knew my brother well. What do you see
  in this?

MACDUFF No foul purpose. Except in Seyton.
  He sees in your brother what he hides in himself.

                                                   Exit Macduff.

MALCOLM O Donalbain! In these halls of flatterers,
  a brother's love is what I long for most—

yet what, as king, I am least safe to have.
If the witches had foretold that I'd
be king, then would there still sit such unrest?
Are not ten years enough to kill the flame
of speculation? . . . Not even in myself.
As king, I mock their prophecy; as man
and witness, I cannot forget. I do
fear Fleance, but that I do my men
can never know; I do suspect Donalbain;
Seyton and Siward have lately grown too bold;
and Norway is not as still as I pretend.
O, unstable anniversary!
I am enthroned by right, but not by fate—
and fate is yet the stronger of the two.
Why then, I shall challenge fate.
What's done can be undone; what's proclaimed,
proclaimed again. What better way to quell
a prophecy than with another?
I shall find the witches, and if by right
am I king, what prophecy can form
but one triumphant, filled with omens fair?
Fleance, I need not net you with my men—
old ladies' words will do the work as well.
What they've spun for you, they'll spin for me.
Head I there with alacrity.   *Exit Malcolm.*

SCENE III

Witches' place.

Enter Malcolm.

MALCOLM This mist of hell confounds. Swore I the hags
lived in this place; yet days of searching bear
no fruit. Perchance times of prophecy
have long since concluded.

Enter Three Witches.

FIRST WITCH Hail to thee, King of Scotland!

SECOND WITCH Hail to thee, Thane of Cawdor!

THIRD WITCH Hail to thee, master of Macbeth!

MALCOLM Can it be? Hear me, sisters. I have come—

FIRST WITCH You speak when you should listen.

SECOND WITCH You listen but hear not.

THIRD WITCH You look but see not.

MALCOLM Do not declaim in riddles. I beseech, if nights
of prophecy have not been stopped,
then I, as king, command: lend me your clouded
vision and ope my fate. O agents of darkness!
Grant me a prophecy to slay Macbeth's.
Speak for me a future, one greater yet
more permanent; one grander yet more secure.

ALL Triple, triple, toil and trouble,
   fire burn, and cauldron bubble.

FIRST WITCH Look to Ireland; from there will hail
   your sorrows. An army shall your brother march
   through the shades of Birnam Wood.

SECOND WITCH Look to the black church: you will love
      Macbeth,
   and love in marriage will divide.

THIRD WITCH No man can kill you but Cawdor.

MALCOLM Stay, imperfect speakers! Stay!
   Pronounce more clearly! I demand!   *Witches vanish.*

MALCOLM They have sunk again into the bog;
   yet their evil residue remains.
   O Donalbain! Would you march a troop
   'gainst your other half? I will prepare.
   A black church? Love Macbeth? Nonsense—
   I cannot love a ghost. None can kill
   me but Cawdor. There is the heart of it.
   Being Cawdor I shall not attack
   myself. Thus am I secure
   in what can never be. See, Banquo,
   you were wrong: your seed shall not sow kings.
   I alone am king!   *Exit Malcolm.*

SCENE IV

Ireland.

Enter Ross, Donalbain and Soldiers.

ROSS Hail to thee, Prince Donalbain!

DONALBAIN It warms my heart to see a living thing
from Scotland. Ireland is now my home,
yet the Highlands sit deep in my heart.

ROSS Sire, is this why you have amassed
these men, which were absent when last we met?
Have you your brother's throne set in your sights?

DONALBAIN Art thou mad? Ha! Nonsense! Indeed!
My brother sits as rightful king; my seat
lies in the shadow of the throne. Gladly so.
For I have studied the missteps of Macbeth
and thus have settled here in Ireland;
unreservedly, then, my brother can rule,
free from the threat of Duncan's other half.
The second-born brother must prop the first. That
is why I have gathered these men.
We have received ill news of Norway's approach.
She means to catch sweet Malcolm unaware,
as a violent storm upon a peaceful sea.
Grace be to God we have netted this scroll. *(hands him scroll)*
                                             Read
how it commands one ship to meet the other.

I shall not rest whilst my dear brother lies
in danger. I have thus lev'raged my purse to recruit
this loyal throng. We shall soon sail for home,
and lend our lives to him.

ROSS I am thus more shamed by the news I bear.

DONALBAIN A message?

ROSS   From your brother.

DONALBAIN   Out with it.

ROSS He is suspect of your intent, and demands
    a private audience.

DONALBAIN Suspect? Of a brother?

ROSS   I shame to speak.

DONALBAIN Suspect? Of his flesh?

ROSS   Your prolonged absence,
    and now this sudden army—they have grown
    as thorns upon his reason.

DONALBAIN   Others prick
    too, I'm sure: Seyton, Siward?

ROSS I do not deny. For he is flocked by men
    of little trust, and in you, the wayward prince,
    they have found a subject.

DONALBAIN The too-worn walls of Dunsinane, soaked
    with evil and disturbances past, are no
    place for a king to sleep. My father's ghost,
    perplexed by a life stopped short, mingles with those
    of foul Macbeth and his wicked queen.

No castle wall, no parapet or porter's
gate could contain these spirits' malcontent.

ROSS Nor that of his living counsel. Forgive
me, sire, but they, though not spectral, do shame
the underworld.

DONALBAIN   Then Malcolm lies in danger
of himself.

ROSS   I do not dispute.

DONALBAIN Then we shall save him from himself. We'll
convince him to leave Dunsinane
and elsewhere build a holier seat;
we'll urge him soon to marry; and we'll purge
him of his treacherous flock. Our men,
meanwhile, shall deter Norway's assault.
Come, we kill the time.

ROSS   I fear how Malcolm
may start when he first sights your men. But I
stand at your side. I once left Lady Macduff
in haste; on my very heels she was slain.
Never again shall I a friend abandon.
I will help you execute whatever
noble device you choose.   *Exeunt.*

SCENE V

Dunsinane.
Malcolm, seated, with Macduff, Suitor, Suitor's Father and Attendants.

SUITOR'S FATHER My liege, my daughter would make the
finest bride in all of Scotland. Her beauty is sung of—

MALCOLM It is apparent.

SUITOR'S FATHER Thank him.

SUITOR Thank you, my lord.

SUITOR'S FATHER My lord, she is a most obedient and de-
voted subject, and would—

MALCOLM Would you like to speak?

SUITOR I am yours, my lord.

MALCOLM Thank you for gracing us with your beauty and
charm. We shall call on you.

SUITOR'S FATHER My lord, 'twould be such an honor—

MACDUFF We shall call on you.   *Exit Suitor and Suitor's Father.*

MALCOLM What think you, Macduff?

MACDUFF   She's fine of form,
and her eyes shine with intelligence.
She would make a fine bride for Scotland.

MALCOLM I am not certain. If it were—

Enter two Messengers, followed by Siward, Seyton, Lennox and Angus.

MESSENGER ONE   My king,
your brother has breached our shores.

MESSENGER TWO   He doth approach
with army fierce.

SIWARD   Traitor!

SEYTON   Villain!

MALCOLM   From whence?

MESSENGER ONE Through the shades of Birnam Wood.

MALCOLM   *(aside)* Thus comes
the prophecy to pass. Yet I'll be touched
by none but Cawdor.

MESSENGER TWO More, my lord. Ross rides at his side.

MALCOLM What, Ross?

ANGUS   'Tis not possible.

SEYTON   'Tis treachery!

LENNOX Rush not to judge. Ne'er was Ross's honor
held in doubt.

MACDUFF Ross would not raise a hand
against your throne. Perhaps they come in peace.

SIWARD What? An army come in peace?

SEYTON   My lord,
  I have heard your errant brother means
  to petition for a title.

MALCOLM   Title? What title?

SEYTON As you already claim that of king and hold
  no need for titles lesser, Donalbain aims
  to acquire "Cawdor."

MALCOLM   *(aside)* Can it be? Is not
  all Ireland enough? Sisters: your riddles
  twist to life. Birnam Wood would mark
  the way. So it does. Only Cawdor
  can harm me. So he aspires. Is there no pause
  between prophecy and consequence?
  No gestation for augury?
  Is the world below more expedient?
  Or did my very summoning create
  the act? Would I had never visited
  that bog!

MACDUFF My lord, I pray you, patience—

SEYTON   Patience? Whilst
  an army advances?

MALCOLM   Patience is a luxury
  not suited to every time. I summoned my brother
  for a private audience; I must
  then view his outward show of arms in but
  one light. I love my brother dearly—yet
  it seems that not all love is requited.

The prince forgets, he is no seed of Banquo.
He is but the second-loved brother,
who must now be first to die. Forgive
me, Father: to save one son, I must
kill your other.   *Exeunt.*

SCENE VI

Birnam Wood.

Enter Donalbain, Ross, Soldiers.

DONALBAIN How deeply this Scottish air stirs me. 'Tis
    mighty strange.
    Never have I felt as content.

SOLDIER ONE   Nor I
    as lost. I can't recall such ghastly fog.

ROSS 'Tis like the very breath of hell.

DONALBAIN   I think
    we are in Birnam Wood, but know not for
    this vapor.

ROSS   Sire, we are. See there? The fog
    begins to lift.

SOLDIER TWO So it does.

SOLDIER ONE   And look!
    Now the sun.

DONALBAIN   Such a sudden shift
    of light I have not ever seen.

ROSS   Sire!
    Look there! Your brother.

DONALBAIN   So it is! May God
be blessed. How it warms my heart to see
my flesh again!

Enter Malcolm, Siward, Macduff, Seyton, Lennox, Angus and Soldiers.
The two armies stop before each other.
Donalbain dismounts, as does Malcolm. The two brothers approach each
other on foot. Donalbain reaches for a scroll.

DONALBAIN Dear brother!   *Malcolm stabs him. Donalbain falls.*

DONALBAIN   Alas! Am I slain by my self?
Now I know why I felt contentment here:
it is to be my resting place. What better
place to die than at a brother's side.
If to be killed by a hand so close, 'tis safer
not to live at all.   *Donalbain dies.*

ROSS Shadow of Macbeth! What vile act
is this? Your noble brother approached in peace,
and you met his embrace with murder.

MALCOLM   He reached
for his sword; I answered with mine.

ROSS   He reached
for a scroll!

                         Ross dismounts, and takes a scroll from
                         Donalbain's hand and hands it to Malcolm.

ROSS He brought you news of Norway's attack. He brought
you men to help defend it!
                    Malcolm reads, and sinks to his knees beside Donalbain.

ROSS   You have killed

the better half of Duncan. *Ross remounts.*

ROSS You have won
the day, but not the time. You now outrank
this friendly group, but Donalbain shall be
avenged. On that day you will earn his blood.
Lennox, with Soldiers, rides to Ross's side.

LENNOX I am with Ross! *Angus, with Soldiers, rides to Ross's side.*

ANGUS And I!
Exeunt Ross, Lennox, Angus and all their Soldiers.

SIWARD My liege, they flee! We must pursue!

SEYTON We must
strike now, before their army multiplies!

MALCOLM What a cruel and callous butcher am I.
Dear, dear brother. How I missed your face
e'en as I struck; I watched my hand perform
the deed e'en as I wished it wouldn't. O, Donalbain!

SEYTON My lord, the fog returns. We must pursue!

MALCOLM The sisters thus speak true. Donalbain
has vanquished Malcolm, worse than a thousand Norways.

SIWARD My lord—

MALCOLM Peace! There will be no more death
on this day. More days will follow, if none
with any worth. *Exeunt.*

SCENE VII

A graveyard.

Enter Malcolm, who sits beside the corpse of Donalbain.
Enter Woman.

MALCOLM Nothing now can harm you further. Not
the slings of fortune, not the touch of a brother's
love. I will have you borne to Colmekill
upon a thousand gilded horses; no place
more befits, for more a king are you
than I. I, a coward who wears a crown,
a crown planted in haste, loosed by our father's
death. On him it should have stayed; then,
on you. For what grants me the right? Being
firstborn? What virtue lies in that? What hand
had I in that? We 'magine that by this custom
a second brother is the lesser; yet this day
proves otherwise.
"I to England." "And to Ireland I."
If only we'd switched paths that fateful day.
You would now be Scotland, and these hands, so tainted,
could be free of fratricide. If only
we'd avenged our Duncan while in restless
death he lay; if only we'd looked more deeply
into the bloody deed. But we forsook
our father's lonely corpse, and on ourselves
drew suspicion. "Our separated

fortune shall keep us both the safer." Not safe
enough from a brother's embrace. "Where we
are, there's daggers in men's smiles." Would
I had greeted you with such a smile.   *Throws his sword.*
What's there? A phantom? The ghost of my mother, come
to rebuke? No, it is too serene. . . .
Sirrah!

Enter Attendant.

Inquire what lady stands thither.

ATTENDANT   Yes, my lord.   *Attendant rushes off, and returns.*

ATTENDANT   She would not give her name.

MALCOLM   Would not?

ATTENDANT   "'Tis a name not to be given,"
   is what she said.

MALCOLM   Not to be given? What sort
   of mystery is this? Who dares not give
   what at birth was given free? Inquire
   whom she mourns.

ATTENDANT   Yes, sire.   *Exit Attendant.*

MALCOLM   Uncanny sight. Such beauty in such a place.
   Such beauty anywhere!   *Enter Attendant.*

ATTENDANT   My lord, she would not tell.

MALCOLM   Not tell?

ATTENDANT   She said,
   "It is a private matter."

MALCOLM   Private? Whose death
  can be so private? Are we not all catalogued
  in that great book of heaven and hell? Is not
  one's absence on this globe so duly noted
  that privacy 'scapes even the most unloved
  of souls? Cryptic woman! So beautiful.
  So solemn. Such a mix I have ne'er seen.
  Perchance she is a seraph, dispatched to test
  my welcome. Then, as Abraham, I shall
  not delay.   *Malcolm approaches.*

MALCOLM My lady, I beg, why
  do you speak so?

WOMAN   Why do you inquire
  of what is no concern to you?

MALCOLM   Death
  concerns us all.

WOMAN   Some more than others.

MALCOLM   How does
  it you?

WOMAN It did not until some threescore weeks
  ago. 'Twas then I was informed of both
  my parents' deaths, and have come here to mourn
  for them.

MALCOLM What, the death of them both?

WOMAN On this very day.

MALCOLM   Bloody anniversary!
  But how did you not know sooner?

WOMAN   My home
is a monastery, far from the news
of the world, and from these parents I never
met.

MALCOLM Never! Alas! But this should make
their death the slighter.

WOMAN   Or heavier. Sometimes
'tis better to know a thing than to wonder
what's been missed.

MALCOLM *(aside)* This lady's words distract.
Forgive me, Donalbain; my heart, so filled
with grief, now wells with something else.
                         (to Lady) Whence
came you?

WOMAN   From the black church. On the isle
of Iona.

MALCOLM Black? How so?

WOMAN   So named for the
garments of our nuns. It is thought
to be God's chosen color.

MALCOLM   You rebuke me with
the mention.

WOMAN   Of God? How so? 'Tis a blessing,
not a rebuke—unless you have rebuked
Him.

MALCOLM O! I have. There lies the corpse

that was my brother, rendered thus by
this very hand.

WOMAN   O! Most horrible Cain!

MALCOLM I knew not he came in peace.

WOMAN   How could
a brother come otherwise? How heavy a sin
you have committed. You must atone.

MALCOLM   I desire
nothing more. But, lady, I do not espy
the graves of your parents. Perhaps we were
acquainted.

WOMAN   I pray not.

MALCOLM   Pray not? Wherefore?

WOMAN I've been told that it was safer to be
from them distant.

MALCOLM   Safer? How so?

WOMAN   My lord,
press no further. I have come to grieve
in silence.

MALCOLM   Art thou an apparition come
to rebuke? I spy no graves here, save for that
crooked cross marking the pit of the Macbeths.

WOMAN I have spoken, my lord.

MALCOLM   Tell me at least
your name.

WOMAN   For what purpose?

MALCOLM   Purpose? Need I
purpose? Know you not that I am king
of all this land?

WOMAN   Titles do not sway
me. There sits a greater king than you.

MALCOLM Greater than me? Who? England? Ireland?

WOMAN The Lord who has made you.

MALCOLM *(aside)* Her piety pierces my soul, rubbing salt
on a heart freshly torn. O bitter
physic! I should leave her; and yet I cannot
tear away.
(to her) Lady, I must know your name.

WOMAN   It is
a name I cannot speak. For so uttered,
it would split the air asunder.

MALCOLM   Then write it.

WOMAN The letters spelt would burn the parchment.

MALCOLM   What name
could do such harm when it doth name so beauteous
a thing?

WOMAN   I pray you, good day, my lord.

MALCOLM   Stay!
As king, I command.

WOMAN   I am not your subject.

MALCOLM You tread on my soil.

WOMAN   A cemetery
  belongs to the dead. Are you king of the dead?

MALCOLM Answer! Answer, I say!!   *He shakes her.*

WOMAN   You have already
  pronounced.

MALCOLM   Pronounced? I? How? Do not
  speak in riddles!

WOMAN   Pronounce again, so please
  you. The crooked cross stares back.

MALCOLM   Macbeth?
  How does this concern you?

WOMAN I am their issue.

ATTENDANT What! Ho!   *Attendant rushes off.*

MALCOLM A child? Of Macbeth?

LADY MALCOLM   I wish that it were other.

> *Enter Seyton, Siward, Macduff, various Nobles, Guards,*
> *Attendants, and a Crowd.*

SEYTON Can it be?

SIWARD Another Macbeth?

CROWD 2 She's much too beautiful.

CROWD 3 Far too humble.

CROWD 4 Yet her age is right.

CROWD 5 I spot Cawdor in her eyes.

CROWD 6 Is't true?!

ALL CROWD We demand to be satisfied! Speak!

MALCOLM Speak, my lady. Is it true?

MACBETH   It is.
   I have been branded with a name in which
   there is no hope for penance.

NOBLES Cursed seed!

CROWD 1 Stone her where she stands!   *Malcolm draws.*

MALCOLM Back! All of you! You'll take no action
   but by my command.

MACDUFF   My lord, we must
   at least imprison. She is an enemy
   to the state. If we do not, this mob,
   or some other, will tear her apart.

SEYTON He speaks wisely, my lord.

MALCOLM Take her to Dunsinane. Secure her in the tower.
               The Guards carry her off, and the crowd cheers.
                        Exeunt all but Malcolm.

MALCOLM Imprison her, I shall, but only that she
   not flee. My wife have I found, another
   Macbeth or no.   *Exit Malcolm.*

ACT · II

SCENE I

Tower. Dunsinane.

Enter Macbeth, in her cell.
Enter Malcolm, in the shadows.

MALCOLM *(aside)* Can she sit so content in such a place,
as if this worldly setting held no threat?
See how her lips move; how she kneels
so softly upon unyielding stone, as if
repenting for every soul in Dunsinane.
Such prayers must go unanswered whilst I inhabit.
My descent to Hades is set, the only question
being the time of my arrival. Satan:
you shall have your prize. But not yet.
For whilst she lives I too have cause to live.
See how she floats to the window, as a bird to light.
Hark! She speaks.

MACBETH The hangman tightens his tool with alacrity,
and the crowd thickens to watch me swing. They think
they'll take my life; but it was long since took
with news of my unholy origin.
If, as the Bible proclaims, our parents' sins
spill over generations, then 'tis best
that they stop here, lest I, by my progeny,
should pass them down again. Ambition is foreign
to me; never have I pined for power
or pearls. Our monastery did not afford

the chance, its vaults stowed with naught but dreams
and prayers. Yet perchance the propensity
sits in my blood. If so, better I hang
now, and be punished for sins still uncommitted.

MALCOLM *(aside)* My lady, your virtues are so true they shame
this Cain to lurk in your shadow. You've siphoned
the best of the Macbeths, your nature proving
their sins came not by blood, but by earthly
lusts. I wonder if you've mistaken your birth.

MACBETH I dreamt that I would die in that very
place. Dreamt I, too, of this cell: such stone,
a door of equal height, a window as this.
Except my illusioned window held no bars,
and in that dream was I set free. A Joseph
delivered to Pharaoh. How imperfect a vision
this was.   *Malcolm unlocks the door and enters the cell.*

MALCOLM Yet perfect enough.

MACBETH Whence
came you? Stood you there all the while?

MALCOLM   I own
the key.

MACBETH Eavesdropping does not become
a king.

MALCOLM Such speech does not become a Macbeth.

MACBETH It was a speech meant for mine ears alone.

MALCOLM Then grace be to God that I was present.

MACBETH   Have you
   not finished mourning your dear brother's death?

MALCOLM   Your virtues compound my grief.

MACBETH   Tomorrow you'll have
   more cause, when I'm hanged for public display.

MALCOLM   I can stay your execution.

MACBETH   If God
   desires it be stayed, it will, by you
   or by some other agent. If He desires
   otherwise, then I am content.

MALCOLM   I knew
   your mother and father. Too well. I cannot imagine
   you are their issue.

MACBETH   'Tis not a name I would
   claim otherwise.

MALCOLM   You never met them?

MACBETH   I was delivered to the nuns newborn.

MALCOLM   But why?

MACBETH   I've wondered at this myself, but have
   not found the cause. Perhaps I was a hindrance
   on their road to ambition. Perhaps
   they had no love for children.

MALCOLM   'Then why mourn them?

MACBETH   If not I, who?

MALCOLM   But why now? Their death
  was ten years past.

MACBETH   It is fresh for me,
  deaf to Scotland's news until my nuns
  deemed fit to share it.

MALCOLM   But 'twas a perilous journey
  for a woman alone.

MACBETH   Nuns pilgrimage
  to far Jersualem; 'twas but a trifle
  beside that.

MALCOLM   If released, will you
  return to Iona?

MACBETH   If God has me released
  I cannot imagine a life elsewhere.

MALCOLM   Then allow
  me to imagine for you. My lady, I am
  in love. . . . Have you no reply?

MACBETH Forgive, my lord. I know not what to say.

MALCOLM Say it is requited.

MACBETH   Requited? How?
  I've never loved a man, and what I know
  of you points to less than that—taker
  of your brother's life, warder and would-be
  executioner of my own self.
  How should I love thee, exactly? What words
  would you have me speak? Riddles and affairs
  of love are not my currency. I've not

been taught the false nothings and idle flatteries
of love's language, have not been reared in the ways
to cloud desire, to twist metaphor and meaning.
And if, my lord, you know already the words
you long to hear, why not recite them to
yourself, hold out a polished glass and mock
my voice? What need you of a living thing
to ape what you can with ease imagine?
It is not requited. And if it were,
I would have no extravagant way
to frame the words, have no device to gild
my syllables, but only say, I love you.

MALCOLM Those words I long to hear, not by my voice
but by yours, for love a single voice
cannot create. The witches said I would love
Macbeth. I knew not what it meant until
this day.

MACBETH Speak not to me of witches. They are
things of darkness.

MALCOLM   They tricked me to take
my brother's life; yet they also led
me unto you.

MACBETH   And now you are a murderer.

MALCOLM Please, use not that word so freely.

MACBETH   You'll needn't
hear it soon enough, as I shall be
silenced by the gallows.

MALCOLM   I shall arrange
  your release.

MACBETH   Upon what condition?

MALCOLM   None. As I am king.

MACBETH   Then I shall humbly
  thank you and take my leave. What, my lord?
  Why do you block the gate?

MALCOLM   Every woman
  in Scotland has petitioned me to marry.
  Do you scorn what others crave?

MACBETH   I crave
  naught but piety, which I'll not find in a murderer's
  arms.

MALCOLM   You know me only as this. Before
  today I was a wise and valiant king,
  who dearly loved the brother he so rashly
  slayed. O Donalbain!   *Malcolm weeps.*

MACBETH   'Tis a heavy deed you have committed.
  Yet penance is possible for all of God's children.

MALCOLM   Then there is hope?

MACBETH   There is always hope.

MALCOLM   E'en for my hand?

MACBETH   I am not a queen,
  my lord. I would not crave the title.

MALCOLM   'Tis why
  it should be yours. I pray you, my lady, consider

what I propose: Scotland needs an heir.
If you desire penance for your parents'
past deeds, then you have found the place. You need
not love me yet. Just take my hand in marriage
and let time teach the rest.

MACBETH   'Tis folly, my lord.
Would you have your subjects convert their most
hated villain into their beloved queen?

MALCOLM My people are but an extension of my will—
they shall be pleased by that which pleases me.
My lady, I vow to repent deeply my actions
past; to renounce all violence; and to
ne'er again seek the witches. I will
become the king I was.

MACBETH My life was took with the news of my
unhappy origin. You would wed but an empty
shell.

MALCOLM They say that shells encase the secrets
of the deep. I'd rather such shell than the
oyster-laden pearl.

MACBETH   Then, as you will.   *They kiss.*
                                                        Exeunt.

SCENE II

Dunsinane.

Enter Malcolm, Macduff, Siward, Seyton and Attendants.

MACDUFF My lord, she must be hanged! Stand you by
whilst a Macbeth is here set free?

MALCOLM   I
am king, and she is free.

SEYTON   My liege, Macduff
speaks true. Our soil is still stained by the reign
of the Macbeths. If the past the future paints,
this rose you now release will one day show
its thorns, pricking not just you but our
entire court.

MALCOLM   The key's long lost; she roams
freely. Further, she is now my guest
in Dunsinane. I've given her parents' quarters
to her, and you shall know that I mean
to make of her my queen.

SEYTON   Queen!

SIWARD   What!

MACDUFF Queen Macbeth!

MALCOLM   "Lady Malcolm" shall she
be called—not Macbeth.

SEYTON   How will the people
   abide?

MALCOLM Have they not hoped for an heir?
   Now they can be content.

MACDUFF   An heir—
   not a Macbeth!

MALCOLM   A Malcolm.

SEYTON   Have we then ousted
   the parents only to grant dominion to
   the seed?

MALCOLM By this royal act the growing
   multitude distresssed over my brother's
   death will also be distracted. Including
   myself.

SIWARD   Donalbain defied your
   decree and breached our shores with brandished arms.
   Sure as he stepped foot on Scottish soil,
   death became him.

MALCOLM   Say again, traitor,
   and you will hang. My brother shall be enshrined
   as the hero he was; a statue is being erected
   as we speak. He died a hero; it shall
   be spoke no other.

MACDUFF   Do you think it wise,
   my lord, to let a Macbeth gain control
   of half the throne?

MALCOLM   Kings control thrones,
  not queens.

SEYTON   Then to let the bloodline of Macbeth
  be heir to Scotland's throne?

MALCOLM   Evil does not
  always come by blood.

SEYTON   Yet evil of such
  proven depth cannot filter with ease.

MALCOLM The prophecy for succession lies in
  the seed of Banquo, not Macbeth. I see
  no harm thereby. Therefore, occupy
  yourselves with the preparation. We marry
  tomorrow: Saint Andrew's Day.

MACDUFF   Think you now
  the most opportune time for
  a wedding? Norway prepares.

SEYTON   And we shall lose
  the chase with Lennox, Angus and Ross.

SIWARD   We must
  stop them before they reach the Irish shore.

MALCOLM I have spoken. Go to.   *Exeunt all but Macduff.*

MACDUFF My lord, if you recall that fateful day,
  'twas I who found your father's bloody corpse,
  carved cruelly at the hand of a Macbeth.
  No seed of such a monster can be pure.

MALCOLM When you found him, did you know it was
  the work of Macbeth?

MACDUFF   I suspected thus.

MALCOLM Yet I knew it the moment the bell tolled.
    We fled; yet you remained.

MACDUFF   I was not certain.

MALCOLM But I was. Just as I am now; and just
    as you again are not. You have proved
    a wise and loyal friend; but counsel me not
    on the nature of my Lady Malcolm.
    Go to.

MACDUFF *(aside)* I cannot abide while he
    builds a ladder for a Macbeth's ascent.
    If too clouded by love to guard himself,
    then I must for him. I will confont
    the evil offspring, and dissuade her from
    this place. If not, I'll bring a dagger, and perform
    the task myself. Better I should hang,
    than Scotland slowly strangle.   *Exeunt.*

SCENE III

Seyton's castle.

Enter Seyton and Syna.

SYNA Marriage! To a Macbeth!

SEYTON   Calm, my child—

SYNA Calm! Calm! Malcolm is mine! By your word,
   I am set to marry! Not to be
   passed over for a harlot from Iona,
   a fake monk stealing into Dunsinane
   to snatch away my ring! I will be queen!

SEYTON Malcolm had never consented to your—

SYNA *I* had consented! What need I from him?
   You pretend to have his ear. Fool!
   You have only influence enough
   to make a mockery of your own flesh:
   to see me, your own issue, thus debased.

SEYTON I did not—

SYNA   Or are you so powerless
   you cannot sway a feeble king to glance
   at your own seed, to behold the best beauty
   in his land?

SEYTON   I petitioned many

times. He promised an audience. But not
to wed. He was against marriage—

SYNA   Against!
Against! He is clearly *for*. Just not
for you.

SEYTON   There is little I can do.
He is set to marry tomorrow.

SYNA   Never
shall sun that morrow see! What, do you
plan to sit idly by and have
a stranger make your daughter husbandless?
Make you bereft of royal lineage?
Have you lost all desire for the crown?

SEYTON I have desire—

SYNA   Then act on that desire!

SEYTON I have tried. He is resolved.

SYNA   You've not
tried hard enough. Malcolm cannot marry
a corpse.

SEYTON   Do not speak thus. Suspicion of
the deed would fall on us. Malcolm, unhinged,
would then never marry. I have a better
way. I know a certain nurse who,
for a sum, will attend our newfound
queen, and report to me her private doings.
I can then inform our Malcolm of his lady's
true intent, and thereby convert him 'gainst

his false beloved. Then you, my willful Syna,
will I present to him.

SYNA   A fair plan.
   I begin to calm. But what if this
   nurse finds no evil in this ugly,
   villainous thing?

SEYTON   Better to find in her
   an ounce of the real thing; but if there's none,
   why, we shall create. I know just
   the woman: a servant who suffered greatly by
   the hand of Macbeth. But, my daughter, if we
   should fail—

SYNA   We fail? How your weakness sickens
   me! You are Syna's father. Act
   in kind! Fail me again, and I shall tell
   Malcolm of all your machinations, and see
   you hang, e'en if my head rolls with yours.
   The queen's throne lies in my grasp; I shall
   not rest until it's mine.   *Exeunt.*

SCENE IV

Dunsinane. Macbeth's bedroom.
Macbeth, seated. Enter Macduff.

MACDUFF *(aside)* What illusion is this? She sits so soft,
  prayer beads on knuckles white, as if to shame
  me for holding this hidden means of death.
  But I must not steer from the required course.
  And surely she feigns. No Macbeth would e'er
  embrace a rosary, unless to pray
  for greater treachery.
                (to her) Lady Macbeth.
  Or shall I dub thee Lady Malcolm?

MACBETH For a few hours more I am Macbeth,
  yet you may dub me as you wish.
  Who, pray, are you? Why such silent entrance?

MACDUFF I am Macduff, husband of the slain
  Lady Macduff, father of the boy
  Macduff: all my pretty ones, all
  butchered by your parents' hand.

MACBETH   Alas!
  Reports of their tyranny do not
  seem to cease. I will include your child
  and lady in my long list of abridged souls.
  I pray for your forgiveness.

MACDUFF *(aside)* Is such piety practiced? Is she more skilled
  in the art of deception than even her parents?
  I will out her yet.
  (to her) You needn't pray on your father's behalf.
  I've already sent him to Hades, dispatched
  him with this very sword: I am the man
  of no woman born.

MACBETH   A Gabriel
  sent to an unrepentant Sodom.
  As my father's taker, I cannot offer
  you my thanks; but as courier of the One
  above, I will accept your decree.

MACDUFF *(aside)* What? Does not e'en this taunt her to true
  color? 'Tis unnatural to not show
  the least sign of enmity. I falter
  in my resolve. Out with it, then.
  (to her) Lady, to the point: as I have known
  your father and mother both too well, I know
  you better than you know yourself. If you
  truly be their issue, then we need only
  wait 'til the day you hatch and subvert us all,
  when your latent ambition will, and must,
  reach beyond these castle walls. To prevent,
  I demand you take your leave at once,
  and tell our Malcolm you will not marry. For to
  protect him is my sworn duty, and by
  my honor, I shall not allow him to
  be vanquished by one so close.

MACBETH   You perform
  your duty well. Would that I had such

a trusted friend. Yet I cannot concede.
I answer only to the Lord above,
and I do now believe He has put
me here to atone for my parents' sins.

MACDUFF Have I slain your father only to kneel
to his seed?

MACBETH   Kneel not to me, but to God.

MACDUFF I stopped kneeling the day He took from me
all that was dear: my whole life stole in one
fateful missive. All I have left is a hardened
heart, and guilt for my cowardice. O!
Would that I had stayed!

> *Macduff weeps. Macbeth rises from the throne and embraces him.*

MACBETH   O terrible fortune!
Most foul Macbeth. Detestable thy name!
A name I'll change in a few hours more;
yet I do not think a simple service
will wipe clean the sins of my lineage.
If punishing myself would lessen your
great loss, I would it gladly undergo.

> *Macduff reaches up to embrace her, and his knife falls to the floor.*
> *Macbeth backs away.*

MACDUFF O my lady! Forgive! 'Twas a dagger
meant for you—a dagger I shall never use!
Now I see that thou art not the stamp
of thine own parents, but a true seraph.
Punish your would-be murderer: if thou
desirest now my hanging, I shall hasten
to the gallows.

MACBETH   I desire nothing
  but the lifting of thy guilt.

MACDUFF Can it be? I'm shamed to the neck.
  Thou art my true, sworn queen; I vow to serve
  thee ever after. If I could not protect
  Lady Macduff, at least I can shield you.
  What a fortunate king Malcolm shall be!
  What a fortunate land Scotland!   *Exit Macduff.*

MACBETH Not as fortunate as thou dost think.
  I spoke to Malcolm that I'd ne'er known love,
  and 'twas true. Yet not anymore:
  Macduff, thou hast educated. It is
  a wisdom I wish I lacked. O faithless queen!
  O Dunsinane! Can your walls so quickly corrupt?   *Exeunt.*

SCENE V

Dunsinane. Courtyard.
A lavish wedding ceremony.

Enter Malcolm, Macbeth, Macduff, Siward, various Nobles and Attendants.
Enter Nurse.

NURSE Such ceremony stands me right on edge.
　　Good flowers torn to shreds; 'twill be a mess
　　to clean. And flower girls, dressed in such finery:
　　frivoling the time when they could be
　　at home, mending clothes and scrubbing floors,
　　as I did at their age. When I was wed,
　　no one came to gape. My husband paid
　　but half a pence, and they cheered us with a pint
　　of ale. Such was our marriage ceremony.
　　No flowers lived in that place; no silks or brocade,
　　as I was the only lady there.

Enter Seyton.

SEYTON 'Tis an odd turn in events. I cannot
　　recall in kind. But yesterday this rabble
　　cried for her head; now they cheer her crowning.
　　Art thou studied on the business to be done?

NURSE But look: how they lavish her with sparkling
　　jewels, promote her with a royal crown.
　　When I was married, I was handed a stick

to beat back fleas, crowned with a net to hold
back lice—

SEYTON   I say, nurse, art thou clear?
For I will not part with this treasure 'til you
parrot back my purpose. If not, I'll find
another.

NURSE   Clear? Why, yes, of course: clear
as a day in Scotland when the fog lifts, clear
as a—

SEYTON Nurse!

NURSE   The business is simple enough.
I will attend our newly minted queen,
present myself as nurse to her, and use
this pretense to catch her words and malign
her to the king.

SEYTON   To me. You will report
to me. You'll not report to Malcolm 'cept—

NURSE Yes, yes, clear enough.

SEYTON   And if you witness
no vices, what then?

NURSE   Then I shall encourage.

SEYTON And if without success?

NURSE   Then I'll invent.

SEYTON Thou art artful in thy craft.

NURSE   'Tis hardly
a craft demanding art. For treachery

is our oldest profession. One need summon
naught but instinct, that warder of the brain,
and let it freely work. Besides, I hardly
lack for motive: Lady Macbeth daily
used me as her whipping thing. She carved
these scars upon my back; still not satisfied,
she turned then to my daughter, and had her lynched
for spying. I vowed revenge yet never it fulfilled.
In death I cannot touch the mother; but here
her daughter I can reach. Revenge so imperfect
imperfectly sates, yet satisfies more
than none at all.

SEYTON   Here's the purse. Perform
  your business quickly. We cannot allow this vine
  to take its root too deep, past the point
  we cannot extract.   *Exit Seyton.*

NURSE   You needn't tutor me,
  old man. I am so practiced in my craft,
  that this new queen comes as a lamb to slaughter.
  She shall meet her new nurse—and crave physic
  thereafter.   *Exit.*

ACT · III

SCENE I

Dunsinane. Queen's chamber.
Lady Malcolm, seated on throne, with Attendants, and Nurse.

Enter First Petitioner.

FIRST PETITIONER Your Majesty: I petition for my mother.
Our estate was seized at your parents' hands, and we live
now on but a portion of what we once were. I have tried to
entreat the king but cannot gain audience. God bless you
for seeing me on this auspicious day.

LADY MALCOLM Where is the plot?

FIRST PETITIONER By Edinburgh, near the sea. My mother is
frail, and the reinstatement of this place where she was
born would grant years more to her virtuous life.

LADY MALCOLM Have you proof of your claim?

FIRST PETITIONER Here, my lady. *Hands her scroll.*

LADY MALCOLM So it reads. I shall petition the king
on your behalf and urge him to set
wrongs right. Please pardon my parents' faults.

FIRST PETITIONER God save the Queen! *Exit First Petitioner.*

NURSE (*aside*) What's this? A fair Macbeth? The ears
deceive.
Surely it is for show; she'll tear that scroll

when the moment suits. O graceful cunning!
True compatriot!

Enter Second Petitioner.

SECOND PETITIONER Your Highness, if your gracious spirit
would extend to yet another, I entreat you hear my case.
The jewels you wear about your wrist were hewed by myself, a gift for my daughter on her wedding day. Your
mother spied them on her way to court and claimed them
as her own.

LADY MALCOLM A daughter bereft of a wedding jewel!
Forgive. Have you proof of what you claim?

SECOND PETITIONER Here, my lady.   *(hands her scroll)*
Signatures of fivescore villagers who witnessed my
furnishing of the bracelet. Here, too—   *(hands her a jewel)*
—a jewel not included. You can see from the fashion it
could have been made by no other.

LADY MALCOLM So it is.
     Lady Malcolm takes off the bracelet and hands it to Second Petitioner.
SECOND PETITIONER Heaven forfend I should deprive you
of your wedding gift on your wedding day! I do not mean
to take that which is already yours, but to ask for recom-
pense in some lesser form.

LADY MALCOLM It is an ancient tradition to hear petitions
on a nuptial day, and thus you do
me more service. I would not wear this bracelet
for half the world. Accept it, please, with
a humble plea that you my mother pardon.

SECOND PETITIONER God save Her Highness! Most noble
  Macbeth!   *Exit Second Petitioner.*

NURSE *(aside)* Even so? O royalty! How well
  thou sits when not driven by base desire.
  Much have my eyes seen, but such displays
  of justice I could not predict. I waver
  in my resolve. Then for the sake of my
  dead daughter, I shall offer jewels which no
  woman can reject, and therein begin
  the lady's corruption.

LADY MALCOLM As we have now concluded a long line of
  requests, I ask that you all leave me. Retire,
  please, to your own rooms, and there attend
  to your own needs. I have no need for servants.
                        Exeunt all Attendants, but Nurse.

NURSE My lady, it seems there is one piece of business
  that you have missed.

LADY MALCOLM   Which piece?

NURSE   Why, the crown.
  Why did you thrust it off so soon? I've brought
  it here to regain its rightful seat.

LADY MALCOLM   Thanks,
  dear nurse, but I am content unadorned.
  I've no desire for such frightful ornaments.
  Pray, return the crown to its storage
  place, from my sight hid.

NURSE   But,
  my queen—

LADY MALCOLM Is there yet more?

NURSE   Why, the very
  scepter of your mother. Borne for centuries
  by Scottish queens, it never left their side.
  'Tis fit that you now brandish it, in display
  of regal privilege.

LADY MALCOLM   My privilege lies only in God's
  good grace. I pray you, store this with the other,
  there to remain until beckoned by one
  more regal-like. Now, good nurse, I pray you,
  leave me so that I may execute
  the evening's prayers.

NURSE (aside) 'Tis not possible. But yesterday I had
  been certain 'twas a just mission; now
  in her I see the likeness of my own daughter.
  O wretched task! To avenge the one I must
  harm the other. Alas: I am yet but young
  in deed.
  (*to Lady Malcolm*) Pray let these ornaments stay for just
  this night, so that the people do not see
  the honors of your royal office disdained
  on their initiation day.   *Exit Nurse.*

LADY MALCOLM Would I were uninitiated still.
  Such sights did not move me a day before.
  O hideous crown! Stare not at me so.
  Pray God, let me look elsewhere; for whilst
  in such proximity it sits, I cannot
  ignore.   (*Lady Malcolm approaches and touches the crown*)
          Thou dost feel like any other

metal; yet thine elements run deep. Too deep,
I fear, for a novice queen. O!
Macbeth! Can one simple jewel change thy nature?
O! Iona! Where hast thou gone?   *Exit.*

SCENE II

Dunsinane. Dining hall.

Enter Malcolm, Lady Malcolm, Macduff, Seyton, Siward,
Syna, Nurse, various Nobles and Attendants.

MALCOLM Friends, nobles. Tonight we raise a glass
unto the resurrection of Macbeth:
a new Macbeth, more virtuous by far
than would the name imply. A true queen
for our land, and a lady I beam
to call wife. To Lady Malcolm!

ALL To Lady Malcolm!

MALCOLM Fortune smiles upon the heels of such
unhappy prologue. Reports spread fast of our
queen's virtues, and the land begins to brim with cheer.
We shall vanquish imprudent Norway, and I
will yield to Scotland heirs!

ALL Hear, hear!

MALCOLM My queen? Add you to the general speech?

LADY MALCOLM Your speech does me too great a service.
  Naught
is fit to add, but only to subtract.

SYNA Surely, our newfound queen, you can bolster
your husband's words?

LADY MALCOLM A husband's words do not
  need bolstering, nor should a lady presume
  to amend.

MALCOLM   Well spoken. A day to mark all days.
  I only wish it were not marred by the death
  of my dear brother. Sirrah!

ATTENDANT Yes, my lord?

MALCOLM   How stands my brother's statue?

ATTENDANT The sculptors work on it throughout the night,
  as you have instructed.

MALCOLM   Add a score
  more to their company.

ATTENDANT   Yes, my lord.   *Attendant exits.*

MALCOLM To my beloved brother, who died a hero's
  death.   *They raise their glasses and drink.*

MALCOLM A drop has fallen on my cuff.
  It settles, see. It will not wash for all
  the world.

          Enter Ghost of Donalbain. Malcolm stares, frozen.

MACDUFF Your highness?

LADY MALCOLM What is it, my lord? Why stare you so?

MALCOLM 'Tis not possible.

MACDUFF Why do you gape at but a vacant seat?

MALCOLM Vacant? Vacant!? If so, then half the world

is uninhabited. Speak, brother!
Rebuke me, as befits.   *Siward draws.*

SIWARD   What, Donalbain?
Where?

MACDUFF My lord, you invent.

MALCOLM   Speak,
dear brother: chastise me in your rage.
What? Not even this? Not a word for
your former self?

LADY MALCOLM My lord, you are unwell.
I pray you—

MALCOLM   What, Duncan, too? His crown
still crooked, blood pouring from his wounds. Forgive
me, Father: I have erased your better half.
What, Macbeth, too? And his lady?
What a bloody feast is this! Ghouls
aligned to hate one more ghoulish than they.
Vacant! Ha! This table is too full.
'Tis yours. I'd rather sup in the midnight air.   *Exit Malcolm.*

LADY MALCOLM I pray your patience. My lord is exceedingly
      tired.   *Exit Lady Malcolm.*
                                                Exuent others.

SCENE III

Balcony.
Malcolm, pacing.

Enter Lady Malcolm.

LADY MALCOLM My lord? You are unwell.

MALCOLM   I shall never
be well, so long as I wear this blood
of Donalbain's. See, it won't come out.

LADY MALCOLM 'Tis not your brother's blood, my lord.
    'Tis but
a drop of wine.

MALCOLM   Then what a potent drop
it is! I will not set foot in that room
again.

LADY MALCOLM Nor need you, ever.

MALCOLM   I begin
to calm, with you here by my side. This night
air does me rightful good. Already the scene
begins to lift.

LADY MALCOLM You are well in health
but not in spirit. I charge you: light a candle
for your dear brother, and join me in my nightly
prayers. Tomorrow we'll to the chapel, where you
can make rightful amends.

MALCOLM   Cawdor alone
  can touch. But I am he.

LADY MALCOLM   My lord?

MALCOLM   I must
  know how it ends.

LADY MALCOLM   What ends, my lord?

MALCOLM   Why,
  my life. Or, rather, Cawdor's. They spoke of Birnam,
  and so it was. They spoke of Ireland; from there
  he came. They must amend my prophecy!

LADY MALCOLM Heaven forfend! Did you not vow to ne'er
  see them again?

MALCOLM   An oath I made in haste.
  I needs must know that I cannot be touched.
  Forgive, my love: their drug sits deep. I crave
  yet one last dose.

LADY MALCOLM   Vile creatures! Satan's
  puppets! I pray you, do not break your vow
  on our wedding night.

MALCOLM   I will promise
  other things, and those I will keep.
  Hark! The bell invites. We will have other nights.

                                        Exit Malcolm.

LADY MALCOLM I fear not as many as we may wish.   *Exit.*

SCENE IV

Witches' place.

Enter Malcolm.

MALCOLM This place is too cold for hell. Cursed
sisters! Where hide you?

VOICE   Here, Malcolm!

MALCOLM A voice! As the breath of a demon
crossed with a dog's. From whence came this? The fog
my vision blinds.

VOICE   Descend, Malcolm!

MALCOLM   The trail
leads down.

Cavern.

MALCOLM What place is this? 'Tis darker than the depths
of night.

Enter Three Witches, with torch.

FIRST WITCH Hail, King of Scotland!

SECOND WITCH   Thane of Cawdor, hail!

THIRD WITCH Hail, Malcolm, who shall be touched by no
man
but Cawdor!

MALCOLM *(aside)* Again do they speak thus. I feel settled
already.
(to them) No man, say you?

FIRST WITCH   Bid us summon our devils
and you shall know further.

MALCOLM   I bid you.

Enter First Apparition.

MALCOLM What awful illusion is this?
It squirms as a snake, yet wears the head
of a man-child.

FIRST APPARITION Fleance will attack.
But you shall find him first.   *Exit First Apparition.*

MALCOLM Find him first? Then I'll stop him!
What else have you, ladies? I bid, summon!

Enter Second Apparition.

MALCOLM What's this? A horned helmet with no face?

SECOND APPARITION Norway shall invade,
but will not win. You shall
be greater than she, yet lesser.   *Exit Second Apparition.*

MALCOLM Greater yet lesser? Strange indeed. Yet Norway
shall not win—'tis all that counts.

FIRST WITCH Are ye satisfied?

MALCOLM Tell me of my lady. . . . Will there be an heir?

SECOND WITCH We bid you not press further.

MALCOLM Summon! I charge you!

THIRD WITCH Thane, some mirrors are best turned round.

MALCOLM I demand!

Enter Third Apparition.

MALCOLM Send it back!
This two-headed beast scorns with a visage borrowed
from my father and brother both! Send
it back I tell you!

THIRD APPARITION Your union shall not last.
Torn asunder it
shall be, by man of no
woman born.   *Exit Third Apparition.*

MALCOLM How dreadful such things exist! Whence
summoned
you this creature?

FIRST WITCH 'Tis not for your knowledge.

MALCOLM Shall not last? Why, 'tis false.
Man of no woman born? Macduff
only. But he would not—
she would not—'tis foolery.
Tell me more!

SECOND WITCH You have overstayed your welcome,
Scotland.

ALL By the pricking of our thumbs,
something wicked this way comes.   *Witches vanish.*

MALCOLM Stay! I charge you, stay!   *Exit.*

SCENE V

Dunsinane. Dining hall.
Seyton, Siward and Macduff, seated.

SIWARD 'Tis as if Macbeth were resurrected.
  I fear he is unwell.

SEYTON Do you fear it? I fear something greater.

MACDUFF   Of what do you speak?

SEYTON Do you think such a sudden shift in nature
  hails unprovoked? That it hath no tutor?

SIWARD Pray, who?

SEYTON   Why, our new queen.

MACDUFF   'Tis false.

SEYTON Her nurse informed me of a plot—

MACDUFF   Villain!
  You lie! Lady Malcolm is the very portrait
  of virtue—she will not be touched. The cause
  of Malcolm's malady lies in his sudden
  grief.

SEYTON 'Tis as I heard.

MACDUFF   I will not hear
  more of this. And speak not of it further.   *Exit Macduff.*

SIWARD A defensive soul.

SEYTON Perhaps he and the queen each other know
    too well?

SIWARD   Think you?

SEYTON   Why else so heated o'er
    a stranger?

SIWARD   I hadn't thought.

SEYTON   Be sure, the queen
    doth stand behind Malcolm's descent. Morn
    'til night she whispers in his ear, stirring
    him to greater ambition.

SIWARD   What greater
    ambition for a king?

SEYTON   Why, the safety
    of that kingship.

SIWARD   By what means?

SEYTON   The removal
    of all too close.

SIWARD   What!

SEYTON   Why else would Lady
    Macbeth orphan her child?

SIWARD   I hadn't thought.

SEYTON To ensure the safety of the Macbeths. She knew
    her fatal games could bring her early death

and thus stowed her seed in reserve,
that it might sprout whene'er the time was right.

SIWARD O most treacherous lineage!

SEYTON   And when
this new Macbeth has fulfilled her plan,
Malcolm will have us buried far beneath
the ground, Then she will poison Malcolm—
as did her mother gracious Duncan—and claim
the throne alone.

SIWARD   Ignoble scheme! O true
heir to Macbeth!

SEYTON   Shall we wait for that dreadful
day?

SIWARD Never! Still crave I vengeance
for the murder of my young Siward. Since
her father lives no more, she can do
the trick.

SEYTON   Then listen close, and we will oust her yet. *Exeunt.*

ACT · IV

SCENE I

Dunsinane. Malcolm's chamber.

Enter Malcolm, by window.

MALCOLM O Donalbain! Your statue rises tall.
Stare not so marble-eyed upon your brother.

Enter Ghost of Macbeth.

How, say you? Why, 'tis not your throne.

Exit Ghost of Macbeth.

What, gone so soon? Macbeth, thy spirit taunts.
Each morn thou perches owl-like on this sill,
only to depart as sudden. The dead should not
be granted such choice of place.

Enter Ghost of Banquo.

What, Banquo, too?
You join in this parade of ghosts, yet I
was not your taker. It is the walls of Dunsinane
that have trapped you.   *Exit Ghost of Banquo.*

Then I am alone.
Duncan and Donalbain dare not alight;
I am too low for such high souls to see.

Enter Macduff, Seyton, Siward, various Nobles and Attendants.

SIWARD My lord, Fleance's men have swelled and now
do brandish arms.

SEYTON   They've massed on our Scottish
  shore and prepare the jump to Ireland. They'll join
  with Ross and mount a joint attack.

MALCOLM *(aside)* Fleance attack?
  Can the witches speak so expedient?
  I have become the puppet king, pulled
  on strings of prophecy. A fruitless crown
  have they placed on my head, teetering
  in the winds of prediction.

SIWARD We must net this threat unto your throne,
  before it gains by doubled strength.

MALCOLM   Macduff?
  Have you of late attended my wife?

MACDUFF   No,
  my lord. I've only met with her once, before
  your wedding, that I might satisfy myself
  of her nature.

MALCOLM   Indeed? And were you satisfied?

MACDUFF Quite. She is a model of virtue.

SIWARD   My lord,
  we waste the time. We must stop Fleance!

MALCOLM *(to Macduff)* What think you of Fleance?

MACDUFF   As before:
  the boy is barely yet a man, and poses
  no real threat unto your throne.

MALCOLM   I'd rather

around me such men than those
too ripe with manhood.

MACDUFF   My lord?

MALCOLM   You seem keen
to let young Fleance go.

MACDUFF   Keen only that you,
supreme king, be sparing in your display
of armed strength.

MALCOLM   We have let Fleance roam
long enough. But I'll not send an army
to net a boy. He can be taken by
a few brave hands. I know just the men:
the very three villains who took his father's
life.

SEYTON Pray, my lord, send not such lowly
creatures to perform a soldier's work. They missed
Fleance already once, and the fate
of the throne must not rest in their hands.

MALCOLM The fate of the throne? What concern of yours
is this?

SEYTON Why, 'tis your fate too, my lord.

MALCOLM The seed of Banquo is only a threat if you
believe the witches speak true. Do you, Macduff?

MACDUFF So it seems, my lord.

MALCOLM   True in all
matters?

MACDUFF So it seems.

MALCOLM   Well then, you
  have spoke it. Ho, thee!

                    Enter Attendant.

                    Summon those three men
  waiting outside my door.   *Exit Attendant.*
                    Now leave me.
                    Exeunt Macduff, Seyton and Siward.

MALCOLM He admits the witches speak true, and thus
    concedes
  his own betrayal. O! Treachery
  so close!

                    Enter Three Murderers.

ALL My liege.

MALCOLM You are the three that stopped the life of our
    dear Banquo.

FIRST MURDERER By King Macbeth's command.

MALCOLM He spoke of you.

SECOND MURDERER Who, my lord?

MALCOLM Why, Banquo. What, speak you not?

THIRD MURDERER He is in heaven, my lord.

MALCOLM Then heaven is not far from here. There is
    another who needs sending. It is his son.

FIRST MURDERER Worm of trickery!

SECOND MURDERER He 'scaped by a mere hairskin, my lord.

THIRD MURDERER The father fought well, to distract us
from the son. A quick little boy was he, with a quicker
horse.

MALCOLM Because of you, this bane of prophecy
has remained a thorn in Scotland's side.
Now you can right your misstep and conclude
the task you failed before.

FIRST MURDERER 'Twill be a privilege, my lord.

MALCOLM He prepares his jump to Ireland.
Move quick. Let Scotland down again, and you
will hang, I swear. Go to.   *Exit Three Murderers.*

MALCOLM Thus tomorrow the prophecy shall end.
If there lies no other seed of Banquo—
and 'tis certain Fleance is the only one—
then none other can claim my throne.
Yet what of Macduff? Did not the sisters say
he would divide? Macduff has been a loyal
friend. But too many types of loyalty
are able to comingle in a single person,
allowing the friend who saves my life to also
seduce my love and find no contradiction
in the work, no breach of the word "loyalty."
Yes, Macduff. I see your plan. Why else
let Fleance abscond? Why, to see me toppled
and clear the way for yourself. Already
he's chopped off one king's head, and is well-practiced
in the art. He is, after all,
a man of no woman born, and such

a man can ne'er be trusted. Very well, then:
on this day I'll settle all accounts,
and give Fleance company in his descent.
Tonight I shall greet Macduff in his sleep,
and reunite him with his loved ones.   *Exit.*

SCENE II

Scotland. Forest.
Fleance and Fiona, seated.

FLEANCE Would this day were as my love, for then
'twould never end; 'twould keep its face turned to
the sun, so that it never set.

FIONA   My love
would stop the sun entire, hold it in
its place so that a day would ne'er again
be marked by a division.

FLEANCE   Alas! Night
falls slow but thick, and we must make for
the ship. I pray you, my lady, come with me.

FIONA Ireland is a strange and foreign
shore.

FLEANCE But we shall be together. All else
is geography.

FIONA   But my family
here resides, and my departure bars
return.

FLEANCE We shall build a family of
our own.

FIONA   As we could in Scotland, if
you'd stay.

FLEANCE   While the tyrant Malcolm reigns,
my days are marked by danger. He's slain a loving
brother—how shall he treat a 'magined threat?

FIONA Then why not seize the throne, and live in peace?

FLEANCE The throne is the least peaceful place
in Scotland.

FIONA   But 'tis rightfully yours.

FLEANCE   By prophecy.
Not by right.

FIONA   Prophecy has run
the course of Scotland since Macbeth did claim
it as his crowning tool. It is as much
a right as any.

FLEANCE   I have no desire
for the throne, and have no ambition
for the walls of Dunsinane. Perhaps
I would claim, if I felt the pull
for kingly power or earthly gain. But I
do not. I possess already all the jewels
our earth can hold; for you have filled my
desire for aught else. So: I pray you,
come with me. 'Tis unsafe here. We must
make to the ship, and I cannot abscond
until you will consent.

FIONA   Would you force

me to decide between abandoning
my love and relinquishing my kin?

FLEANCE Which love's the stronger?

FIONA They cannot be compared.

FLEANCE The last light of sun doth darken my heart.
  'Tis clear now that you mean to stay.

FIONA   I'll come.   *They kiss.*

FIONA But I must first take leave of my kin.

FLEANCE They'll not assent.

FIONA   My mind's made up.

FLEANCE   We haven't
  time. My men wait for us.

FIONA   Go
  to them. Inform of my near arrival.
  I'll to my family and bear the brunt
  of their tearful departure.

FLEANCE   I like it not.
  The night grows thick. I pray you, join me now,
  and let us be done with Scotland.

FIONA   I will
  not flee like a thief in the night. I must
  look one last time upon their faces.

FLEANCE Then my hours will be heavy with waiting.

FIONA This will keep them lighter.   *They kiss.*
                                            Exuent.

SCENE III

Scotland. Forest.

Enter Three Murderers.

FIRST MURDERER Again the fate of Scotland twists in our
hands.

SECOND MURDERER Then 'tis good they are murderers'
hands—broad and thick, and deep in the palm.

THIRD MURDERER If you think rightly, 'tis not just Scotland
but the entire world, Scotland being the seat of civilization.

FIRST MURDERER Then we are the bearers of civilization.

SECOND MURDERER No Scottish king, it seems, can thrive
without our services. Then why not be kings ourselves?

THIRD MURDERER We'll carve Scotland three ways.

FIRST MURDERER I'll take Fife.

SECOND MURDERER I, Edinburgh.

THIRD MURDERER I, Glasgow.

FIRST MURDERER A triumvirate.

SECOND MURDERER Like Caesar and Antony and—who
was it?

THIRD MURDERER Cleopatra.

FIRST MURDERER 'Twas not Cleopatra.

SECOND MURDERER Hark! Here comes one.

Enter Fiona.

THIRD MURDERER It must be the lover of Fleance.

SECOND MURDERER Why then, 'tis like netting the boy
   himself.   *The Three Murderers confront her.*

FIRST MURDERER No further!

FIONA Who's there?

SECOND MURDERER A friend.

THIRD MURDERER Three friends.

FIRST MURDERER Where is your lover, the would-be boy
   king?

FIONA Fiend! He's in a place that you're too low
   to find.

SECOND MURDERER You'll speak. Fleance is not the only
   lover in Scotland, as we'll soon educate.
            The Second Murderer grabs her. She strikes him.

SECOND MURDERER My eye! 'Tis lost! O cunning
   harlot!   *He strikes her. She falls.*

FIRST MURDERER Now where hides Fleance?

FIONA He's on his way to Dunsinane, to oust
   your bloody master and seize the throne himself.
   That concluded, he'll next hang each of you
   and rid the world of the stench of your humanity.
            Second Murderer strikes and kills her.

THIRD MURDERER What have you done? She was the bait to lure the bird.

SECOND MURDERER My eye is lost!

FIRST MURDERER Now we all are lost. If we report the loss of Fleance, we'll share her fate.

THIRD MURDERER Then we'll lie. Fleance is dead. We killed him.

FIRST MURDERER We stabbed him twenty times.

SECOND MURDERER Severed his head.

FIRST MURDERER But where is it?

SECOND MURDERER Eaten by a boar.

THIRD MURDERER Snatched from our very hands. Let's smear this blood and pretend 'tis his.

FIRST MURDERER Come, let's leave this bloody scene, and collect our fee in Dunsinane.   *Exeunt.*

SCENE IV

Dunsinane.

Enter Malcolm and Lady Malcolm.

LADY MALCOLM My lord, why rise at such unheavenly
    hour? 'Tis not yet light; the owl still cries.
    Pray, come back to bed.

MALCOLM   'Tis light enough
    for a dreadful deed.

LADY MALCOLM   Deed? Of which
    deed do you speak?

MALCOLM   Of one no man was born
    to do, yet will befit one of no woman born.

LADY MALCOLM What's that you grasp? A dagger? For what
    purpose?

MALCOLM To defend the crown.

LADY MALCOLM   Defend? From what?

MALCOLM 'Tis not for your wholesome ears to know.
    I go alone to make our palace safe.

LADY MALCOLM But 'tis safe. The Lord above protects.

MALCOLM But the lord below provokes.

                       Lady Malcolm kneels before him.

LADY MALCOLM   Mean you
  to commit murder?

MALCOLM   'Tis a word
  too absolute.

LADY MALCOLM Drop this evil guide,
  I pray you, and return to our wedding bed.

MALCOLM 'Tis our union I aim to protect.

LADY MALCOLM My lord, do not commit this heinous sin!
  'Tis a stain upon our souls!

MALCOLM   What?
  'Tis not true. I never touched you, Banquo.

LADY MALCOLM To whom do you speak? My lord, you are
  not well. I pray you!

MALCOLM   Why, here's your mother,
  come to accompany.

LADY MALCOLM   My lord!

                      Exit Malcolm. Lady Malcolm weeps.

SCENE V

Scotland. Forest.

Enter Fleance, with Soldiers.

FLEANCE 'Tis strange. Her parents claim she did not come,
yet she's not met us at the ship. This is
the trail where we last met. No trace at all.
I start to fear some dreadful deed. Spread
further, and raise the lanterns high.

FIRST SOLDIER Here my lord!

Fleance and others discover Fiona's body.

FLEANCE O, cruel and unjust heaven! Here's a sight
to rend the soul. The very visage of
an angel tumbled down to earth, but with
no cloud to stop the fall. O humanity!
How cruel and callous thou art.   *Fleance kneels and holds her.*

FLEANCE 'Twere not for me, thou wouldst be safe, embraced
still by the family thou loved most. The reach
of my destiny runs too deep, harming
all who come too close. Had I heart
left to live, I'd lend it thee, to pump
the blood that flowed so nobly in thy veins.

SECOND SOLDIER My lord, we must make to the ship. These
woods
become unsafe.

FLEANCE   My love, this time you shall
    accompany, and like the albatross,
    lead our voyage. Great Neptune shall weep
    whilst he hosts, and Ireland will greet
    you with profound celebrity.

THIRD SOLDIER My lord, we must depart.

FLEANCE   Woe to thee, Malcolm.
    I who gave my life to love shall learn
    the ways of war; I who worshipped Venus
    will turn my face to Mars.
    "Avenge, thou mayst, Fleance!" Would I had
    abided my father's cry—then thou wouldst live,
    O sweet Fiona. Now I shall obey.
    Vengeance now will be my new companion,
    and vengeance shall breed vengeance unto such extreme
    that violence will but a prologue seem.   *Exeunt.*

SCENE VI

Dunsinane. Macduff's chamber.
Macduff, sleeping.

Enter Malcolm.

MALCOLM Duncan slept in that very bed
when Macbeth did his deed. Am I,
then, too, a parricide?
'Tis strange. But yesterday I had never
dreamed of murder; now this arm that thrust
Donalbain so deep does by its own crave more,
as if all of Hades' minions I've unleashed.
If I could but close the gates, I would;
but I fear the lock's been picked, and the weight
of the world above cannot turn back
the hinge.
Macduff, if I think truly on the matter,
never did me harm; advised me well;
indeed, I never saw him with my wife.
I have become infected with this curse
called power, this insatiable trap
that leads to nothing but wanting more, that turns
our friends to foes, suitors to traitors, brothers
to villains. Even if imagined, our fancies
are real enough, and fancies beget plans,
and plans beget action.
Yet—I had a motive—what was it?
Man of no woman—tear my union—

I cannot recall. The early hour plagues
my memory.
The dagger shakes.
The deed must now descend or else forever
must I forego.
For the sake of our union, then.
Awake, O adulterer!   *Malcolm stabs Macduff.*

MACDUFF Am I stabbed by the one I loved the most?
Rest now, Lady Macduff: thou art avenged.
Rest now, boy: your coward father doth return.   *Macduff dies.*

MALCOLM Forgive me, Father: it seemed I saw your face
when I the dagger thrust. Did I then murder
Duncan? I can't recall.
What a hideous death was this!
So noble was he in the act of dying,
as if to further scold his taker.
The blood has stained my arm entire—
it shall not ever wash out!   *Exeunt.*

SCENE VII

Dunsinane. Lady Malcolm's bedroom.
Lady Malcolm, sleeping.

Enter Nurse and Doctor.

NURSE I tell you, she is not well. I heard
her cry out "murder." She plots some treachery,
just like her mother.

DOCTOR Speech in sleep does not point to the doing.

NURSE I tell you— Hark!

LADY MALCOLM   O king, do not murder!

NURSE There! 'Tis proof!

DOCTOR   She spoke *not* to murder.

NURSE 'Tis but the same—her mind is occupied
with the deed.

DOCTOR   'Tis not the same. She is
a noble and virtuous queen—do not paint
her otherwise. Yet her mind is troubled.
I should attend.   *Doctor wakes Lady Malcolm.*

DOCTOR   My queen, forgive the start.

LADY MALCOLM Is he safe?

DOCTOR   Who, my queen?

LADY MALCOLM   Macduff.

NURSE Why would he be otherwise?

LADY MALCOLM O! What a hideous dream.

DOCTOR   My lady,
   your mind is troubled. I pray you, take as physic
   this root—'twill put you fast asleep.

LADY MALCOLM   Most gracious,
   but 'tis my spirit that suffers, for which no root
   is strong enough.

NURSE   Why so, my lady?
   Answer you not?

DOCTOR   Pray, nurse, leave us.

NURSE *(aside)* Leave you, I shall, but not 'til I finish
   my task. I thought it would be simpler; yet she
   resembles too much my daughter. No matter. I must
   see it through. Farwell, Macbeth.
   If I have my say, tomorrow I'll
   undo thy wedding day.   *Exit Nurse.*

DOCTOR Pray, take this root, my lady. Thou shalt
   sleep well, and sleep shall make thee well.

LADY MALCOLM   'Tis the place,
   I fear, that makes me unwell.

DOCTOR Your mother I also did attend.

LADY MALCOLM What was she like?

DOCTOR Far from your likeness. I am no man of spirit,
   but if I were, I would also point

to this place where your mother lived,
and dreamt as she slept, and walked as she dreamt.
These stones are held by no mere mortar.
As unphysic-like as it may be,
to advise you to hasten from this place
would be the only remedy in my bag.

LADY MALCOLM You have performed your service graciously.
I pray you, leave me now. *Doctor exits.*

LADY MALCOLM He advises too well, and echoes my own
thoughts of late. Malcolm vowed a life
free of blood and witchery—within
these short hours his vows are broken twice.
What worth, then, is a wedding vow?
His murder of his brother, in the heat
of battle, might be a sin forgiven. But
to murder sweet Macduff! In this, he's torn
our union asunder. I shall not
sleep beside a murderer.
On the morrow I will depart this place
and return to my Iona.
O Mother! Would you had never conceived! *Exit.*

SCENE VIII

Dunsinane. Ramparts.

MALCOLM Some water and this arm comes clean; some more,
and so does this. Can murder wash away
so quick? Can murderers keep walking thus,
breathing free, unpunished by their act?
Where has judgment gone? It must lurk in
the afterlife. I think 'tis better, then,
that I live longer here.

Enter Three Murderers.

Yet there seems
no end to the blood that I must spill
to keep my kingdom safe—and keep it safely mine.
What say you, Banquo?
Fleance lives? Yet more blood to spill.

FIRST MURDERER My lord? To whom do you in counsel
speak?

MALCOLM Why, my guide to the world below.

FIRST MURDERER Yet I see none.

MALCOLM Why dost thou return?

SECOND MURDERER We have done the deed.

THIRD MURDERER Fleance is dead.

MALCOLM Which one performed the deed?

ALL 'Twas I—

FIRST MURDERER 'Twas all of us, my lord.

MALCOLM By whose order?

FIRST MURDERER Why, yours, my lord.

MALCOLM Where then is the blood?

>   *Murderers hold out their sleeves.*

ALL 'Tis here.

MALCOLM But 'tis not on my sleeve.

FIRST MURDERER My lord?

MALCOLM Your deed is done. Mine, I fear, is yet to come.

FIRST MURDERER *(aside, to other murderers)* He suffers from
some malady . . . 'twill be short time before he learns
Fleance still lives. Let us quickly flee this place.

>   *Exit Three Murderers, running.*

MALCOLM So. Fleance is dead. Donalbain is dead.
Macduff is dead. And Cawdor does not live,
except in me. Then, there are none left to fear.
Yet still I feel unsafe. Danger, where
dost thou lurk?   *Bell rings.*

VOICE Murder! Murder! Macduff lives no more!

>   *Enter Seyton, Siward, various Nobles and Attendants.*

ATTENDANT My lord! Macduff has been slain!

MALCOLM   Where?

ATTENDANT Where he slept. Three men, garments stained
in blood, were spotted fleeing our castle. Suspicion
falls on them.

MALCOLM   Where is Macduff?

ATTENDANT   My lord?
He's slain.

MALCOLM   But where is he now?

ATTENDANT   Gone
to heaven, I suppose.

SIWARD   My king, we must
pursue the murderers.

MALCOLM   Pursue.   *Exit Attendants.*

SIWARD This castle is unsafe.

MALCOLM   To be safe,
we must be safe from ourselves.
Pursue!   *Exeunt all but Seyton and Siward.*

SEYTON *(aside, to Siward)* Note you not who's absent here?

SIWARD   Who?

SEYTON Why, the queen. How doth she sleep so sound
despite alarums of murder?

SIWARD   I cannot fathom.

SEYTON Why, because she is the root.

SIWARD   She?

SEYTON She has begun erasing all too close

to her throne. If only she'd spared sweet
Macduff! We shall be next.

SIWARD   Star of villainy!
We must inform Malcolm!

SEYTON   In his present
state, he will not hear. Fear not—tomorrow
I'll convince the king.

SIWARD   'Til then. For now, I'll join the chase.
O bloody night!   *Exit Siward.*

SEYTON   O opportunity!
I shall seize thee in confusion yet.
Sweet Syna, prepare thee Scotland soon to wed.
O Seyton! Prepare thee, too, to grandfather kings!   *Exit.*

ACT · V

SCENE I

Ireland.

Ross, Lennox, Angus, various Nobles and Soldiers.

Enter Fleance.

ROSS Our good Fleance. News has already spread
of the tyrant's latest treachery.
Accept our most profound remorse, which comes
with the might of our good men to help
exact revenge.

FLEANCE   Revenge? Too light a word.
It would have been a fitting term after
the murder of my dear father. But with the death
of my love, revenge shall learn new meaning.

LENNOX Surely, though, you will spare the people
of Scotland?

FLEANCE   I will spare none close to Malcolm.
All else shall live.

ANGUS   Well spoken. First among
those are Seyton, Siward—

FLEANCE   First are those
three murderers.

ROSS   Be heedful that our army,
e'en swelled with your brave ranks, remains a fraction
still of Scotland's force.

FLEANCE   'Tis of small consequence.
Fear has fled me since the death of my Fiona.
Caution and temperance have vanished with the loss
of all I loved. I'll happily gallop straight
into the fiercest hordes of the warring world.

ROSS News of Malcolm's malady has spread.
Perhaps his soldiers, deeming his cause unjust,
will part and join our ranks.

FLEANCE If not, our ranks will do.
Better to die defying a tyrant than
to live in fear of one.

LENNOX   Look! The heavens
light a celestial streak.

ANGUS   A sign. It marks
the fall of a king.

FLEANCE   And the rise
of another. To the ships!   *Exeunt.*

SCENE II

Dunsinane. Ramparts.

Enter two guards.

FIRST GUARD 'Tis awful strange. The heavens churn, as if battling with each other.

SECOND GUARD Such a night I have not seen.

FIRST GUARD 'Tis almost daybreak, yet 'neath such stars, the day seems near broke.

SECOND GUARD Does not sit well for Scotland.

FIRST GUARD Think you?

SECOND GUARD When the stars cross just so, bodes the death of a saint.

Enter Ghost of Macbeth.

SECOND GUARD You there! Stand to!

FIRST GUARD Do not come closer!

SECOND GUARD Look! He floats!

FIRST GUARD Why, 'tis King Macbeth!

SECOND GUARD He tries to speak but cannot!

Exit Ghost of Macbeth.

FIRST GUARD O hideous night!

SECOND GUARD Never have these ramparts needed more
guarding—and never have we been less equipped!   *Exeunt.*

SCENE III

Dunsinane. Malcolm's chamber.
Malcolm, seated.

Enter Seyton.

SEYTON The hunt advances for our lord Macduff's
  three murderers. They should be caught by midday.

MALCOLM Is this a day which breaks outside
  my window? Why streaks the light a bloody red?

SEYTON 'Tis but a sunrise, my lord.

MALCOLM   Does not bode well.
  Fleance is dead, yet still I am not safe.

SEYTON You seem safe enough.

MALCOLM   Another seed
  of Banquo must hide far in the land.

SEYTON   Closer,
  I fear.

MALCOLM What say you?

SEYTON   Nothing, my lord. I have
  o'erspoke myself.

MALCOLM   Speak again. Now, sirrah!

SEYTON My lord, I should not want to be the cause
  of some misfortune.

MALCOLM   A greater shall descend
if presently you do not speak.

SEYTON   So be it—
but pray you, do not then direct your wrath
upon the one conveying. A certain nurse
has of late approached me and has confided
misgivings about her lady. She has discovered . . .
intentions on your throne.

MALCOLM   A lady? My throne?
Who, pray? Who? Speak!

SEYTON   Your queen.

MALCOLM   What!?
Lies! Treason! You shall hang! Guards! Guards!

SEYTON My lord, I vow, 'tis true. She was heard plotting—

MALCOLM Guards!

SEYTON   And aims to avenge her parents—

MALCOLM   Guards! Ho!

SEYTON And claims that she is rightful Cawdor!

Enter Guards.

MALCOLM   What? Cawdor?

FIRST GUARD My king? We crave your bidding.

MALCOLM Cawdor, say you? My queen?

SECOND GUARD   My liege?

MALCOLM   Go to.

Exit Guards.

SEYTON She was heard claiming her father's title. She
    'magines
  she is Cawdor, and by this right can seize
  your throne and rule Scotland alone.

MALCOLM Can it be? One so close?

SEYTON   I speak true,
  my king. I have the nurse who will avouch.
  She waits outside the door.

MALCOLM   Fetch her.   *Seyton opens the door.*

Enter Nurse.

NURSE My liege.

MALCOLM Speak truly, woman, or these words shall be
  your last.

NURSE   My king, your lady I've attended
  these several days.

SEYTON   Go on.

NURSE   She owns a face
  of virtue, yet such secret ambition I ne'er
  have witnessed—

MALCOLM   Guards!

NURSE   Upon her entrance she demanded
  I fetch the scepter.

MALCOLM   Scepter? For what purpose?

NURSE So, said she, to test the weight of it.

Before I'd barely pressed it to her palm,
she demanded that I bring her crown.

MALCOLM Crown?

NURSE   She aimed to wear it e'en to bed,
but hid it so that you would not suspect.
And when your royal chamber sat vacant,
she had me lead her thither.

MALCOLM   My chamber? Wherefore?

NURSE To sit in your very throne. Startled
at the sight, I inquired of her motive.
In order, she answered, that she might feel her future.

MALCOLM On this very throne?

Enter Guards.

GUARDS   My liege?

MALCOLM   Go to.   *Exit Guards.*

NURSE She states further that she by birth is rightful Cawdor,
and that you, usurper, are but the lowly
son of a slain Duncan, are but a vain
pretender to the crown.

MALCOLM   Pretender? I?

NURSE She has it in her sights to avenge both
her parents' deaths. Her plan is to finish
you this very night, whilst you lie
in sleep. She's procured a poisoned root,
which sits e'en now beside your bed.

MALCOLM   Enough!
  Be gone! Both of you!   *Exit Seyton and Nurse.*

MALCOLM O excellent treachery! O practiced piety!
  Most true Macbeth! The grandest deceit
  saved for the grandest villain of them all.
  She urged me to avoid the witches. Why?
  So she could not be prophesied against.
  She was the cause of my killing Macduff:
  for her sake did I slay my loyal friend.
  Her father was indeed Cawdor. Yes:
  through this lens, perhaps she is Cawdor, too.
  'Tis now all clear. A poisoned root?
  Alas, dear love, could you not at least
  have used a dagger? Could you not
  have met your eyes to mine in that fatal moment,
  as I did for Macduff, as your father
  did for Duncan? If just one ounce of honor
  had descended this Macbeth line; but no—
  the next of kin have multiplied deceit,
  have learned to mask treachery with most
  expert subtlety.
  O practiced nun! O false monk!
  I'll to our bed and see if such root
  exists. If so, she'll meet her own deathly
  embrace. O most vile treachery!
  O most true Macbeth!   *Exit.*

SCENE IV

Dunsinane. Bedroom.
Lady Malcolm, sleeping.

Enter Malcolm.

MALCOLM There is not light enough for the deed,
    though I do not think light enough exists
    to point the way. Here crawls the sun, and still
    the morning bird is silent, as if forgetting
    night has left.
    Perchance the nurse speaks false. My lady's face
    doth shine with such divinity, I can scarce
    conceive it hides ambition.
    Still, I've heard it said aspirers
    sleep soundest of all. Perhaps 'tis but
    yet another tool in her arsenal
    of deceit. And yet I see no root. Perchance—

                      Malcolm steps on the root.

MALCOLM O violent herb!
    What evil shape your branches take, their reach
    aimed right for me. Patience: your poison will flow
    soon enough. But not in my veins.
    I'll feed my lady this midnight sacrament
    she meant for me, and at least one of us
    will wake absent of earthly worries.

                  Malcolm goes to put the root in her mouth.

MALCOLM   Yet, I cannot. Her mouth so sweetly sleeps,
I dare not feed.
Then I shall use this dagger, raise it high
and plunge it quickly, thus not to think upon
the deed until 'tis done.   *Malcolm raises the dagger.*

MALCOLM   Yet, I cannot. The metal shakes, and for all
the world would not reach her heart.
Then these hands must do. These hands, so stained,
must one last time perform.
                    Malcolm places his hands around her throat.

MALCOLM   Yet, I cannot. The skin is too soft;
these hands could only stroke her face. What then?
Allow my would-be murderer to inhabit
my bed? If I let her live, I murder
myself. Yet I've not the will to be her taker.
Guards!

                    Enter Two Guards.

MALCOLM   Take her away.

FIRST GUARD   Whence, my lord?

MALCOLM   To the gallows.

SECOND GUARD   My lord?

MALCOLM   Do not delay!
            *The Guards grab one arm and pull Lady Malcolm out of bed.
            She wakes as they drag her from the room.*

LADY MALCOLM   My king! Help me!
                    Exeunt all but Malcolm. He weeps.

SCENE V

Dunsinane. Courtyard.

Enter Seyton, Syna, Nurse, Siward, Nobles, Soldiers,
Attendants, Hangman and a Crowd.
Enter Lady Malcolm, blindfolded and dragged to the gallows.

SEYTON Our most treacherous queen, the very mirror
of her mother, here stands charged with conspiracy
against our throne. Therefore, by the king's
decree, we sentence her to death by hanging.
                    The crowd cheers. Lady Malcolm is put on the gallows,
                                        a rope put about her neck.

NURSE *(aside to Seyton)* My lord, I can't stand by. Already
I regret my role.

SEYTON   *(aside)* Be silent!

NURSE   *(aside)* I had
supposed my actions would lead to her banishment
only. My lord, I beg! She resembles too much
my daughter!

SYNA   *(aside)* Speak again, old woman, and my
dagger will speak for you.

HANGMAN   Final words?

LADY MALCOLM I pray that God may heal your souls, and
mine;

and that my parents be remembered as what
they were, not what they had become.

ALL   Hang her!

NURSE   My lady!   *Lady Malcolm is hanged. Crowd cheers. Nurse weeps.*

SYNA   *(aside)* O throne! Thou art but a ladder step away.

FIRST CROWD MEMBER   See, she invoked her parents. 'Tis
certain she was evil.

SECOND CROWD MEMBER   'Twas never any doubt, from the
moment she aspired.

THIRD CROWD MEMBER   Now can Scotland rest.

FOURTH CROWD MEMBER   What's this? The sun is covered.

SECOND CROWD MEMBER   A blot upon the heavens! 'Tis
unnatural!

FIFTH CROWD MEMBER   'Tis said to be thus when a saint
doth die.

Bedroom.
Malcolm watches from the window, weeping.
                                        Exeunt all.

SCENE VI

Scottish shore.

Enter Fleance, Ross, Lennox, Angus and Soldiers.

FLEANCE The fog rolls out to greet us, whilst our ship
　has barely touched the shore. A good sign.
　For the fog is to advantage when
　so greatly outmanned.

ROSS 　　　　　　　　Then Scotland comes to its own
　defense, in helping to oust its tyrant.

LENNOX 　　　　　　　　　　Look!
　In the fog!

ANGUS 　　　What apparition's this?

ROSS It takes the form of your dead father.

FLEANCE 　　　　　　　　　Banquo
　it is, come to greet his wayward son,
　to help conclude what he could not.

ROSS 　　　　　　　　　What's there?
　Behind him!

LENNOX 　　　'Tis an illusion. I spot eight kings.

ANGUS The last holds a glass.

ROSS 　　　　　　　　The sisters thus
　did prophesy. The seed of Banquo stirs.

Enter Cawdor's Son and Soldiers.

ROSS You there! No further.

LENNOX   What sort of welcoming
  party is this?

FLEANCE   By your brandished arms
  it appears you hail in Malcolm's cause.

CAWDOR'S SON   No,
  our good Fleance. Forgive this dangerous show,
  as these arms are but the outward sign
  of our love on your behalf. We have
  come to aid you in your mission.

FLEANCE   Whence
  hail you?

CAWDOR'S SON From a place no son should hope.
  You, sir, have the good fortune to hail from
  an illustrious father, whose cause you champion
  with equal valor. I've a father of
  another kind: alas, his very name
  doth shame the air.

FLEANCE   Speak it, then. Our time
  is short.

CAWDOR'S SON Pray you, by the father do not
  hate the son: Cawdor is my lineage.

ROSS What? Another Macbeth?

CAWDOR'S SON   No. My father
  was Cawdor first, he who betrayed Scotland
  for Norway in our time of need.

LENNOX   A traitor
  was he! Hanged by righteous Duncan.

CAWDOR'S SON   And
  rightfully so. I do not contest.
  Rather, I beseech, good Fleance, give me one chance
  to clear my family's name. 'Tis the only
  name I own, and a father does not
  always a son make.

ANGUS   Do not trust him.
  His father was a treacherous villain.

ROSS Such depth of treachery cannot erase
  in but a single generation. You'd risk
  all our fates to trust one so poor bred.

FLEANCE What do you propose?

CAWDOR'S SON I have here a hundredscore men,
  each one loyal, and each knowing I bear
  no likeness to my father. We offer to
  abet your cause.

FLEANCE   What have you in return?

CAWDOR'S SON Should your grace see fit: to restore
  the Cawdor title to my family.

ROSS Do not be swayed, my lord. For in the heat
  of battle, he will turn, as did his father,
  and ravage us the worst.

LENNOX   A trick or trap
  it could be, contrived together with Malcolm.

FLEANCE I, too, champion my father's name,
though I wish I'd done it sooner. I shall
trust you, for it takes equal courage
to trust as to live, and in these times
we must learn to live again. A son
must not be branded for his father's deceit.
Know you that we stand outmanned?

CAWDOR'S SON   Too well.
But if this day should be my last, then it
will be well spent. The number of our days
matters not if we have no just cause
to fill them.

FLEANCE   Then kneel.

> *Cawdor's Son kneels. Fleance knights him.*

FLEANCE   And rise, Cawdor.
For from this moment you shall wear that title,
in anticipation of your valiant
action on the field this day.

CAWDOR   God bless
your grace. I shall not betray.

FLEANCE   Men.
On this day we fight to set wrongs right,
to oust a tyrant, and restore the throne of Scotland.
Do you wish to live your years in Ireland,
hiding as cowards? Do you wish to live
as exiles, banished from your homes, in order
to appease a tyrant's ambition?

ALL No! Never!

FLEANCE Then ride with me this day. Hold high your swords,
and ever after it shall be recalled
that on this day few fought against many,
and with valor challenged tyranny!

ALL Hail, Fleance! Scotland's rightful king!   *Exeunt.*

SCENE VII

Dunsinane. Courtyard.

Enter Porter. A knocking.

PORTER Knock, knock! Shall this pounding ever cease? If not the wind, then 'tis some lonely soul, thinking he'll find grace behind these walls. Knock, knock! Patience is a virtue lost by all but me. It takes proper time to open a door; 'tis an art missed by those ignorant of the craft. Knock! By my slow tread I make you knock some more, and anticipate the opening. 'Tis what a good porter does: for it is the anticipation that brings the visitor most joy. *Porter opens the door.*

MESSENGER An army comes through the shades of
    Birnam Wood!
    I must to the king! *Exit Messenger.*

PORTER Without me, this door would not have opened, and thus this messenger would not have passed. News would not spread. Armies would not prepare. Ah, the life of a porter! I am the keeper of all there is. An army approaches? I've seen many an army pass by this gate. One will be the victor, the other, vanquished. One day the victor, too, will be vanquished. But I shall always remain. For the victor will always need a door. And that door will always need a porter! *Exit.*

SCENE VIII

Dunsinane. Malcolm's chamber.

Malcolm, seated. Enter Doctor and Siward.

SIWARD He's not moved from this window since the death
of his brief wife. 'Tis as if he's frozen.

DOCTOR He is not frozen; only the thoughts have
within him froze. He is beyond physic.

SIWARD But you must intervene. You are a doctor.
And he is king.

DOCTOR   Even doctors cannot
heal a mind diseased. Our good king
has supped from the root of sorrow; once
ingested, 'tis not quick to leave the blood.

Enter Messenger.

MESSENGER My king! An army doth approach, with Fleance
at its head!

SIWARD   What, to Dunsinane?

MESSENGER My king? Dost hear?

SIWARD   Go to, sirrah!   *Exit Messenger.*

SIWARD   My king!
We must defend! Grant me authority
to summon our men. Merely nod your head—

Enter Nurse.

DOCTOR   What now, nurse?

NURSE   I swear, it was not me.
   'Twas the brutal lady.

SIWARD   Shall maladies
   never cease? She walks as she sleeps,
   and speaks as she walks.

DOCTOR   'Tis the sign
   of a mind disturbed.

NURSE   Forgive me, Lady Malcolm.
   A saint more righteous I'd not seen.

SIWARD   E'en so?

NURSE   'Twas Seyton, and his daughter. You were but
   the stepping stone. I spoke false! O! Forgive!

MALCOLM   False?

SIWARD   The king rouses!

DOCTOR   O unlikely
   physic! One malady heals another.

MALCOLM   Speak again, nurse.

NURSE   Forgive! Malcolm
   has been sore deceived. O forgive!
                    Malcolm rises and stabs her. She dies.

MALCOLM   Prepare my army.   *Exit Siward.*

DOCTOR   My liege, I joy to see
   you roused.

MALCOLM   I do not. Better I had sunk
  unto the depths. O black nurse! Evil Seyton!
  They dragged my queen onto the gallows—whilst I,
  their donkey, was by them led.
  Nothing is but what is not.

DOCTOR   And now?

MALCOLM   If half a man, I'd take my own life.
  I am Cawdor, after all: so who
  more fit? Yet e'en for this, I lack resolve.
  Thus, to Fleance.
  Let his men do what I cannot.   *Exit Malcolm.*

DOCTOR   And I, anywhere but here. Farewell,
  Dunsinane. Your walls I pray to never
  see again.   *Exit.*

SCENE IX

Dunsinane. Corridor.

Enter Malcolm.
Seyton and Syna approach.

SEYTON My king, may I present my daughter—
                    Malcolm stabs and kills them both.

MALCOLM Present her to my Lady Malcolm.   *Exit.*

SCENE X

Witches' place.

Enter Malcolm, Siward and Soldiers.
Malcolm dismounts, carrying the corpse of Lady Malcolm.

MALCOLM Rouse you, hags! Rise up from your foul depths,
and lend me a potion to revive my lady.
Answer, I say!   *Witches' laughter.*

SOLDIER What wretched noise is this! As if the earth
were torn in two.

SIWARD   They mock, my lord.

MALCOLM   Then I, too,
will mock: Cawdor shall not Cawdor take.
I'll see myself slain by some other—
any other—but by myself, and thereby
prove their prophecy false.
Donalbain, be patient: your brother comes to visit!   *Exeunt.*

SCENE XI

Scotland. Battlefield.

Enter Malcolm, Siward, and Soldiers.
Enter Fleance's soldiers. They fight.

MALCOLM Donalbain! Where art thou?

SIWARD   This fog rolls in
    so thick, I cannot see who we fight.

MALCOLM 'Tis the witches' breath, come to confuse.
    You there! Fight your king!   *Malcolm kills a Soldier.*

MALCOLM And you!   *Malcolm kills another.*

MALCOLM   And you!

ROSS   'Tis Ross you taunt.

MALCOLM   Traitor!
    The better for my sword.   *They fight. Malcolm kills him.*

ROSS   Alas! Slain
    by the monster. Donalbain, forgive.
    Thee I did not avenge.   *Ross dies.*

MALCOLM   Donalbain!
    Dare you invoke my brother's name?
              Malcolm stabs Ross's corpse repeatedly.

MALCOLM   Who else?
    Who else shall die by Cawdor's hand? For none

but Cawdor can touch, and on this bloody day.
I shall not kill myself!   *Malcolm kills several soldiers.*

Battlefield. Elsewhere.

FLEANCE You there! Turn and fight!

SIWARD   I shall not fight
  a boy!

FLEANCE A man who is your king!

SIWARD   Worm
  of prophecy! Coward who fled his father's
  death!

FLEANCE Coward who fled his young son's death!

SIWARD Villain! Young Siward died a soldier's death.
  You shall die a traitor's.   *They fight. Fleance wounds him.*

SIWARD Slain by one
  so young! Age, thou art deception.   *Siward dies.*

Battlefield. Elsewhere.

Cawdor kills several of Malcolm's soldiers.
Enter Malcolm.

MALCOLM You there! Art thou ready now to meet
  thy maker?

CAWDOR   Not by your hand. And not today.   *They fight.*

MALCOLM What? My sword does not pierce. What man
  art thou?   *They fight.*

CAWDOR Cawdor.

MALCOLM   Liar! I am Cawdor!

CAWDOR But my father was before you—
and I, after!   *Cawdor stabs and wounds Malcolm.*

MALCOLM   At least in this, the sisters
speak true. My lady, forgive your husband.   *Malcolm dies.*

Enter Fleance, Lennox, Angus and all Soldiers.

FLEANCE Thus the tyrant falls. But our day's work
is yet undone.

Enter Soldiers, escorting the Three Murderers.

FLEANCE   Here stand before us three
of the most heinous creatures e'er to stain
our Scottish soil: these three who murdered first
my father, then Macduff's beloved wife
and son; who took from me my fair Fiona.
Murderers, what say you? Nothing.
'Tis fitting. Then let it come down!
                    Fleance stabs and kills all three. The crowd cheers.

ALL Hail, Fleance! All hail the boy king!   *Exeunt.*

Finis.